Tasha Sings the Blues

ECHO FREER

Other  titles

Magenta Sings the Blues

ECHO FREER

Hodder
Children's
Books

A division of Hachette Children's Books

I would like to offer huge amounts of gratitude to the following people: my husband, Frank, and my daughters, Imogen and Verien, for all their help, advice and support, as well as my agent, Caroline, and editor, Rachel, for all their hard work and input. I'd like to thank Jac Dhillon and Sundeep Deol for the use of their names, and a special thank you goes to Jordan Worton for his brilliant brainwave to call the dhol drummers MaSikhs. I would also like to say a huge, special thank you to my son, Jacob, for his amazing technical know-how on Daniel's music track, and my son-in-law, Dr Michael Kelly, for his knowledge of all things computerified!

Text copyright © 2008 Echo Freer

First published in Great Britain in 2008
by Hodder Children's Books

1

A Catalogue record for this book is available from the British Library

ISBN-13: 978 0 340 94418 9

Typeset in Palatino by Avon DataSet Ltd, Bidford-on-Avon, Warwickshire

Printed and bound in Great Britain by CPI Bookmarque, Croydon, CR0 4TD

The paper and board used in this paperback by Hodder Children's Books are natural recyclable products made from wood grown in sustainable forests. The manufacturing processes conform to the environmental regulations of the country of origin.

Hodder Children's Books
A division of Hachette Children's Books
338 Euston Road, London NW1 3BH
An Hachette Livre UK Company

Dedicated to my late parents:
Margaret and Cyril Sunley
with love xxx

1
Magenta

It's official – my life sucks! And not just a teensy bit either; we're talking a major suck-fest here.

For those of you who haven't been keeping up with the soap opera that is my life – I *used to be* happy. In the days when it was just Dad, Gran and me, things were sweet. We all got on OK – well, as OK as can be expected when you've got a generation gap the size of the Grand Canyon, but still, we muddled through. And the neighbours were friendly too – Mary and her sons Joe and Daniel who live next door. Daniel and I *used to* get on really well. (Note the use of the past tense.) You know the sort of thing: nice platonic friendship; best boy mate etc. In fact I can safely say that everything in my personal little domestic eco-system was chugging along just great!

But then I think I must have been struck down with some mysterious brain bug that caused the whole thing to go out of balance, because I (stupidly) agreed to go out with Daniel. And, believe me, was that one HUGE mistake! Talk about all aboard the emotional roller coaster! In the past year, Daniel and I have been on and off more often than my gran's wig. But, believe me, we are very much *off* now – and this is permanent!

I suppose the beginning of the end came last summer. Daniel was allowed to come on holiday with my family – which I thought was brilliant at the time. Unfortunately, when we got home, he discovered that his house had been totally flooded. (Actually, it was my grotesque grublet of a cousin, Holden, who'd slept round there and accidentally left the tap running – for the whole week we were away! Ooops!)

Anyway, you should have seen the place when we got back; oh my God! Talk about *Waterworld*. Daniel's mum was practically hysterical. The basin had overflowed in the bathroom and water had poured through the ceiling and down into the kitchen. It had soaked through the kitchen floorboards and then started filling up the basement. By the time we got back you needed an aqualung to get into Daniel's cellar and all Mary's kitchen worktops were covered with soggy plaster where the ceiling had fallen down. There was even a mini waterfall cascading out of the front door and down the path. And to make matters worse, the electrics had blown.

So, to try and make amends for his useless weasel of a nephew, my dad (who has always bordered on the insane) offered to let Daniel, Mary and Donald (Mary's new husband) stay with us till their house had been repaired. At the time – because I was obviously still under the influence of sunstroke from our holiday – I thought it was a brilliant idea having my boyfriend around all the time (delusional, or what?) – doing our homework together, eating together, watching TV together. It seemed really romantic – until reality hit!

One minute Daniel was all, 'Oh, you're so lovely, Magenta.' And, 'I really love you, Magenta.' And, 'I don't know what I'd do without you, Magenta.' And the next he was morphing into Dad/Adolf Hitler mark II. 'Don't leave your lipstick on my bed please, Magenta, it might mark the duvet.' (Excuse me?) Or, 'I think you'll find that I washed up yesterday, Magenta – it's your turn today.' (Yeah, right!) And, 'Can't you take your music into your own room, Magenta? I've got coursework to do.' (What!) He seemed to have forgotten that it wasn't *his* bed I was putting my lippy down on. Or *his* room I was listening to music in. It was *my* bed and *my* room that *he* was sleeping in! Honestly! I mean, before he came along and volunteered me as a domestic servant, I hardly ever had to do any washing up. Now Belinda and Dad expect me to carry on doing it even though Daniel's moved back home! Just because Mary treats her kids as slaves, Daniel seems to think that's the norm, and now my family have bought into all that child abuse stuff. It is so unfair – my nails will be ruined because of Daniel.

And he was always on at me about doing my homework. 'Shouldn't you be doing your Maths investigation, Magenta?' and 'Have you finished your English assignment, Magenta?' or, 'Instead of just sitting there, why don't you do some drawings for your Art sketch book, Magenta?' Ggggrrr! I've managed very well so far, thank you very much, without School Master Davis on my case. Doesn't he think I've got enough to cope with at the moment with Dad, half the staff at school and now the Dung-beetle nagging me about homework? By the way, the Dung-beetle is my private tutor. Can you believe it? My Rasputin-like father has sentenced me to a minimum of two years' hard labour every Saturday morning at the hands of Mr Dumbarton (aka the Dung-beetle). He's a retired head teacher with skin like the surface of the Moon and eyebrows that meet in the middle, and his mission in life (which, sadly, he chose to accept) is to get me decent grades. Yeah, right – by boring me to death? I don't think so! What I don't understand is how my ultra left-wing stepmum has allowed Dad to get away with such elitist behaviour. Sending me to a *private* tutor indeed! Not very education-for-the-masses, is it? Hypocrite!

And on top of all that I've had to put up with four months of Daniel polluting my (previously) gorgeous bedroom with his smelly PE kit and his hair gel and his pictures of Ferraris and McLarens everywhere. It was just too much. My gran always says: *You never really know someone until you live with them*. And how true that's turned out to be. So, as soon as the repairs to Mary's house were finally finished and Daniel moved back home – which was only last week – I dumped him! Which is sooooo the best thing that's happened to me since – well, since Daniel and his family moved in with us.

But, before you start thinking that that was the

only reason life sucks at the moment – it isn't. There are many other ways my life is the pits:

As well as having to put up with four months of sharing my home with Dan, Dan the Brown-Nose Man, I've also had to put up with four months of sharing a bedroom with my gran. I mean, how gross is that? A bedroom's supposed to be a place of refuge, right? A sanctuary; a place where I can go to get my head together? But the second the neighbours from Hell moved in and my proper, lovely girly bedroom got infested with testosterone, my temporary bedroom became the last place I wanted to go for some space. Everywhere I looked there was disgusting beige underwear draped all over the place, and when I wanted to put my make-up on, the dressing table was always littered with wax earplugs and tubs of cocoa butter and hairnets and jars of 'cold cream'. (I mean, what *is* that? Is it the opposite of *hot* cream, or what?) I even came face to face with a tumbler of false teeth the other day. Eeewww! It's enough to scar a girl for life. Between you and me, I'm amazed I've come through it with my sanity intact.

On top of that Belinda – my once laid-back hippified stepmum and the voice of reason in this family – has turned into some sort of raving banshee. OK, so I know she's seven months pregnant, and I'm sure she's got lots of extra hormones zooming around her body and everything, but really! There is no excuse for how she's been behaving. You'd think she'd be happy to be having a child of her own. I mean I know we get on really well, and she values me as a stepdaughter, but right now she's snapping at everyone (and me in particular) like a crocodile with PMT. 'Do not leave the pizza box on the settee please, Magenta.' 'Tidy your clothes up, Magenta.' 'Turn your music down, Magenta.' Moan, moan, moan!

But, the worst thing is that my two best mates, Arlette and Seema, both went away for the holidays. Seema's family went to see her grandmother in Delhi for the whole two weeks and Arlette's went skiing. So, when the day came to go back to school, I could not wait.

I was a teensy bit late because I'd gone back to sleep after my alarm went off and Belinda refuses to knock on my door any more. She's got this bee in her bonnet that I have to take responsibility for myself. I always thought she'd be a really cool parent, but actually, this pregnancy isn't doing her any good – and I pity that poor baby when it comes out: she'll probably expect it to be making its own feeds by the time it's three months old.

But anyway, I knew it didn't really matter if I was late because we always have this extra-long registration on the first day of term and Mr Kingston, our form tutor, is sooo laid back. But what I hadn't taken account of was that I wouldn't be the only one who was late that morning.

'Good *afternoon*, Ms Orange.' Eeek! The body of Mr Kingston had been taken over by Mrs Blobby, our head of year and local Attila the Hun look-alike. And, if you hadn't already picked up on the fact, Mrs Blobby speaks fluent sarcasm. 'Good of you to join us. Perhaps you'd care to explain your lack of time management skills to the rest of the form.'

It might be worth pointing out here that Mrs Blobby (aka Mrs Delaney, to her face) is about as much one of my fans as a barracuda is a fan of the mackerel. That is, only when it's eating it for breakfast. In a word, the Great Pink Blob *hates* me.

I put on my most apologetic voice. 'I'm really sorry, Mrs Bl— Delaney but my stepmother is pregnant and she slipped over this morning, so I had to help her up and stay with her to check that she hadn't gone into premature labour.' OK, so it was a bit of a porkie, but Belinda had actually tripped over one of my slippers on her way to the bathroom (and took it out on me – again!), so I was only stretching the truth a teensy little bit.

Mrs Blobby stood there with her hands clasped in front of her, twirling her thumbs round each other. She had a grin like a demonic cat just before it pounces on a poor helpless mouse. 'Interesting,' she said, nodding her head in that *I've got your number* sort of way. 'I seem to recall that your stepmother slipped and threatened to go into labour the day you were supposed to be on litter duty last term.' Ooops! 'And didn't she slip over and need you to rush home from school to look after her when you were supposed to have a detention for Science?' Double ooops! '*And* when you had a detention for PE?' I'm sure it's not normal to have a memory *that* good.

'Erm . . .'

'In fact, Ms Orange, I know your stepmother very well and I think I ought to telephone her and suggest that she see a doctor for this clumsy-itis that she seems to have developed since she finished working at this school.'

You see – this is why I need to keep a notebook and write down which excuses I use for which teachers and when. It would save so many problems.

With that, Mr Kingston loped in. 'So sorry: my motorbike broke down on the motorway.'

But did she give him a rollicking for being late? I don't think so!

'Sit down, Magenta,' Mrs Blobby said as she went out of the room. Phew! I'd got away with it. 'And come and see me at lunch time.' Or not. Oh well, what do I expect? I was doomed the day my dad went and married my ex-teacher. They're all in on the network and are plotting against me. I don't stand a chance of getting away with anything. It's so unfair.

I went to the back of our tutor room but, whoa! What was going on? It seemed to be a Boffins Anonymous meeting back there. Chelsea Riordan and Hattie Pringle, who normally sit right at the front of every lesson, had come to our patch and were sitting with Seema. Of course, it was a relief to see Arlette there, keeping up the side as the token non-brainiac.

'OK, let's hear it.' Arlette was sitting on the table brushing Seema's hair. 'Give us all the gories.' She was looking way too excited about the news that Daniel and I had split up for good.

I pulled out a chair and sat down. She could at least have looked a little bit upset for me, being boyfriend-less again.

'Nothing to tell, really. I suppose I've just grown out of him.' Arlette looked at me in this *yeah-right* sort of way. 'No really, Arl. You have no idea what he's like. And anyway, that's not very supportive of you.' I didn't want to have to remind her of how much sympathy I'd given her when Ben Jestico had dumped her after nearly a year together.

Seema was making notes about something but she said – a bit too dismissively, I thought – 'You'll be back on again, no worries. You and Daniel always are.'

'Not this time,' I said with total conviction. 'It's over – for good!'

'So . . .' Arlette put on this nonchalant voice that wasn't convincing anyone, '. . . does that mean that Daniel's available again?'

'Arl!' I *knew* she still had the hots for him! As if it wasn't bad enough that she'd gone out with Ben the minute Seema had finished with him, she was after Daniel now. Had she no self-respect? Talk about sloppy seconds!

'Only asking,' she said.

'Trust me, Arl, don't even go there. You're worth better. In fact . . .' I'd just had a brainwave, '. . . as we're both free agents again, why don't the two of us go down to the Filling Station on Saturday afternoon and check out what's happening?' Suddenly being single was looking very appealing – especially as I now had Arlette as a partner in crime to go cruising with.

'Erm . . . well . . .' Arl stuttered.

Seema tutted. 'Come on, Arlette. Madge'll understand.'

'Understand what?'

'We're rehearsing on Saturday,' Seema said – just like that.

'Rehearsing?' We'd only been back at school ten minutes – OK, so some people had been back for half an hour – but what could they be rehearsing? Auditions for the school play wouldn't be for a couple of weeks yet and anyway, surely they'd have told me about it. 'Rehearsing for what?'

Arlette looked sheepish.

'Arl? What's all this about?' I was starting to

feel scared. Something was going on and I didn't know what.

Seema turned round to face me. 'Didn't you see the poster in the foyer?'

Yeah, right! I'm late and I'm going to come in through the foyer where the mighty Blob is usually lying in wait for her prey? 'No – what poster?'

Then Chelsea piped up, 'For the Battle of the Bands. We're forming a girl band.'

'The four of us,' Hattie added.

I did a quick head count – Seema, Arlette, Chelsea, Hattie. That made four. And me? Where was I in this four-person girl band that they were forming?

'Oh cheers!' I said. But before I could say anything else, the fire alarm went off. Brilliant! I mean who has a fire drill within half an hour of coming back after the holidays?

'Leave all your things and form an orderly line,' Mr Kingston was saying.

I grabbed my bag and walked straight out of the door. 'At least I know who my friends are,' I shouted over my shoulder. Humph!

So, what a brilliant start to the New Year this has been!

a) The first morning back was spent standing out on the netball courts in the freezing rain – I'm surprised I haven't got pneumonia by now.

b) Not that I could even go to bed to recover because my bedroom is a health hazard that I'm still having to detox after Daniel lived there for four months.

c) One of my favourite people has been body-snatched by a crabby old bag – which, funnily enough, could apply to either Belinda or Mr Kingston.

d) I am, yet again, without a boyfriend.

And now,

e) My so-called friends have decided to form a band WITHOUT ME!

And you thought I was exaggerating when I said my life sucked. I wish!

2
Daniel

Christmas was crap! Magenta was in my face the whole time. Of course it didn't help that Mum and I were still dossing down at her house, so I couldn't even go home to get away from her. I felt like I could hardly breathe.

And New Year was nearly as bad – but in a different way. I always spend New Year at my dad's, but this year Dad and his girlfriend, Pauline, went out to a party leaving me with only my reptilian brother, Joe, and a bowl of peanuts for company when the clock struck twelve. Great! And a happy New Year to you too!

Of course, as the old year went out, so did my love life because the first thing I did once I got back to Mum's – before I'd even unpacked all my stuff – was to go over the balcony and end it with Magenta.

'Now what is it?' she shouted when she looked up and saw me outside her French window.

Old Mrs Pickles across the road was in her front

garden putting paper bags over her prize plants (she says it protects them from the frost: don't even go there) and I didn't really want the whole neighbourhood listening to my private life, so I just mouthed through the glass, 'Can I come in?'

Magenta gave me this look that could've put Mrs Pickles' plants into cryonic suspension even from that distance. 'Why? It's actually been very peaceful round here while you've been away.'

I knew she wanted a reaction, but I was determined not to rise to her bait. I kept my voice very calm and low – well, as low as I could and still be heard through the French window. 'We need to talk.'

But was she going to listen to me? Oh no! Never let it be said that Magenta ever did anything anyone else wanted. She just carried on reading the magazine that was laid out on her bed and put up her hand – like some stupid lollipop lady trying to stop the traffic.

'Sorry, Daniel – this face just ain't listening.'

Then she licked her fingers and started flicking through the pages of her magazine in an exaggerated manner. The annoying thing was, it was so obvious that she wasn't really reading it; she

16

was just trying to make a point. Well, she couldn't complain that I hadn't given her a fair chance.

'Fine!' I raised my voice – who cared if Mrs Pickles heard me or not. 'Your face may not be listening, but let's hope those King Lears of yours are pinned back because – WE'RE OVER!'

She looked up and cupped her hand round her ear as though she couldn't hear me.

'Did you say something?'

Can you believe her? OK – she'd asked for it. 'I'M DUMPING YOU!' I screamed at the top of my voice.

She got up and opened the window a crack and pretended to wipe her eyes. 'Boo hoo hoo! Only, you forgot something, Daniel.'

'Oh yeah?' I said through the narrow opening.

'Yes – you can't dump *me*, because I already dumped *you* – so there!'

Now where did *that* come from? '*You* dumped *me*? Yeah right! Sorry – I must've been sleeping because I missed it.'

She picked up a bright pink notebook from her dressing table and waved it in my face. 'Yes, actually – I wrote it in my diary yesterday.' She flicked through a few pages. 'Oh yes, here it is:

January first – New Year's resolution: DUMP DANIEL!' Then she threw the book on to her bed, closed the French window and drew her curtains.

I was standing on the balcony facing a wall of bright pink fabric, but I wasn't going to give up that easily. 'Get into the real world, Magenta – not everything happens inside your head, and not everybody orbits Planet Madge. *I* am the dump-*er* in all this and *you* are the dump-*ee*. Accept it!'

I turned to go back across the balcony to my own room but Old Mrs Pickles' cat, Geranium, had weaved his way in between my legs and I almost went flying over the balcony rail. 'Aaagh! Get . . .' I was just about to let out some of my frustration on him when I realised his owner was still bagging up her chrysanthemums within earshot. I picked him up and gave him a little stroke instead, waving across the street as a neighbourly gesture. 'Happy New Year, Mrs Pickles!' I called, rubbing Geranium against my face.

But I heard a faint, 'Nah-na nah-na, Mrs Pickles. Brown nose!' coming from Magenta's room.

I gave one more wave and smile to Geranium's owner before putting him down and going into my room. Only I made sure I closed my French windows very, very quietly. No way was I going to give Magenta the satisfaction of thinking she'd got to me. Door slamming is so childish – I hear her doing it through the wall all the time.

In fact the more I think about it, the more I wonder why I ever went out with her in the first place. I mean, she's really immature and, in terms of high maintenance, Magenta makes the Eiffel Tower look like a piece of Meccano. And talk about self-absorbed; it's all Me, Me, Me with her. She couldn't even let me end it without trying to take that away from me too. Like I believe all that rubbish about writing it in her diary – what does she take me for? A total moron?

Anyway, it's over now and I'm relieved. Moving in with Curtis and Belinda was probably the best thing we could've done – as Mum said, at least I found out what she's like now, rather than later. I mean, imagine if we'd gone on for years and I'd never known.

But, though I didn't doubt for a second that I'd done the right thing, I was still feeling low when we went back to school the next day. I was halfway through the foyer before I noticed the humungous poster that had already gathered quite a crowd.

'Hey, Danno.' Magnus ran up to me and slapped me on the back. 'Get a load of this.' He pulled me back to read it.

'Yeah, should be good,' I said, without much conviction.

'I've been thinking,' Magnus said as we walked down the corridor to our tutor room. 'We should enter.'

I've got to be honest, my head still wasn't really thinking straight. 'How can we? We're not in a band.'

'Durrr! You've got to think outside the box.'

I was beginning to think that he'd inherited the stupid gene from his twin, Angus. 'What are you on about, boxes?'

'Think laterally, my furry little friend. Do not be restricted by conventional ideas.'

I stopped. 'Look, mate. It's the first day back. My brain's not even in gear yet. You're going to have to start speaking English 'cos you've lost me.'

'Are we or are we not the geniuses of Music Technology?'

I gave a modest shrug; it was true, we were the best in our set, with A*s for our coursework so far. 'And your point?'

Magnus could hardly contain himself. 'It doesn't say what kind of bands, does it? Not all bands have your traditional rock line-up, do they?'

We'd got to our form room and I slung my bag on to the table. 'Am I missing something here?'

'Only your brain cell, my pedigree chum.' Cheers, way to go on the friendship front. 'Think about it. We could develop that Big Beat track we're working on in Music – especially now you've got Cubase at home.' Dad had bought me some software and a sampler for Christmas so that I can compose music on my computer. 'Then we can add some samples, do a little bit of remixing and ta-dah!'

I nodded my head as I began to see what he was getting at. The idea was sounding more and more appealing. 'And we could have a huge screen at the back and images could flash up in time to the beat.' I could see it all in my head; move over Fatboy Slim.

Magnus was sitting on the back of his chair with his feet on the seat. 'And in Systems and Control we could build a unit so that flashlights can be synchronised with the music and they'll blaze across the stage.'

'And sweep right across the hall as everyone's dancing.'

'It would be wicked, blud!' He flicked his fingers together.

'Think of it – fifty quid each.' Mentally, I was already spending my winnings.

'What's fifty quid each?' Spud asked as he and Angus wandered in.

Oh crump! I felt a bit guilty agreeing to form a band with Magnus before I'd even discussed it with Spud – after all, Spud was supposed to be my best mate.

But before I could answer, Angus butted in, 'Spud told me you'd binned Magenta.'

Oh great, just what I needed – a conversation about my ex.

On some level, it was a relief that he'd taken the conversation away from the band – at least it meant that I might have a chance to break it gently to Spud. Unfortunately, though, he'd steered it in a direction that I didn't really want to go. It was like leaping out of the lion's jaws and into the tiger's.

'Lucky escape, if you ask me,' he went on. Always big on sympathy is Angus!

Then I watched as he pulled a load of bog roll out of one pocket and sat down on the floor, unloaded pebbles from the other pockets and began striking two stones together trying to spark a light and set fire to the toilet paper. So, his spell with the Child and Family Therapist didn't work then.

'What – you two've finished again?' Magnus asked, looking up from the drawings he'd already started on ideas for our band logo.

I nodded. 'I don't really want to talk about it.'

He shook his head and grinned. 'Neh, you two'll be back together again, you always are.'

'Not this time,' I said with total conviction. 'It's over – for good!'

'So . . .' Spud was trying to sound all casual, '. . . does that mean that Magenta's available again?' He was rubbing his hands together till I'm surprised Angus hadn't used them to ignite his tissues. 'If it's OK by you, of course,' he added as an afterthought.

I shrugged. 'You can take your chance if you like.'

'Aw, brilliant,' he said, thumping Angus on the back excitedly and knocking the pebbles out of his hands.

'Oi, leave it out!' Angus snapped.

'Sorry, mate, but . . .' Spud put both thumbs up, '. . . hey, hey! Magenta's up for grabs again!'

I took Spud by the arm and led him to one side, away from the twins. 'Look, mate, I might have dumped her but she's not a prize in a raffle you know.'

'Point taken.' There was a pause. 'But seriously, she's fair game, right?'

I know, strictly speaking, Magenta wasn't anything to do with me any more, but it really pissed me off the way Spud was talking about her like she was an object. I might not be going out with her, but he could at least have shown her some respect.

'Just . . .' I didn't know what I wanted to say to him. Part of me was thinking I shouldn't care who she went out with and yet there was also a part that did care and knew that Spud was to romance what anthrax was to all living creatures. 'Just be nice to her, OK?'

'Hey, Danno,' Magnus called before I had a chance to say anything else. 'What d'you think?' He held up a drawing of a sunburst severed by a bolt of lightning and the word *Luminance* across the middle.

'Wow! It's nang, blud!'

'What is it?' Spud asked.

Oh boy! I needed to do some pretty quick thinking. 'It's our band,' I said. 'Erm . . . Magnus and I are going to do the mixing and stuff . . .' I shot Magnus an apologetic grimace, '. . . and you and Angus will be the teching crew. You know, sorting out the lighting, cables, all that sort of stuff.' Magnus raised his eyes and shook his head. 'And if we win,' I went on, trying to salvage both of my friendships, 'we'll split the prize money seventy:thirty.' I tried to look excited. 'Just think, that'll be fifteen quid each for you and Angus just for humping a few lights and boxes around.'

'Sixty:forty,' Angus piped up from under the table. 'And I'll throw in some fireworks.'

'No way!' Magnus protested.

'Done!' said Spud, shaking my hand – just as Angus's bonfire of bog roll burst into flames.

So, right now, my life blows!

1) I've got a filthy cold because I had to spend half of the first morning standing on the netball courts in the freezing rain without my coat just because the evil twin Angus-the-Pyromaniac was out of rehab.

2) Our tutor group was lined up next to Magenta's and I had to witness Spud sleazing up to her in front of me. Pul-ease, where does he get his lines? A Christmas cracker?

3) Magenta's friend Arlette was coming on to me big time. Not that there's anything wrong with Arlette, but we went out last year and, I'm sorry, she just doesn't do it for me.

4) Magnus is really pissed off with me because, if we do win the Battle of the Bands, our prize money has been reduced from fifty quid each to thirty and he's claiming that was down to me. Like, hello – am I the one

with the psycho-brother? All I was doing was trying to be straight with everyone.

And,

5) We've got exams next week and Mum has decided that it would be a fantastic idea if I went to Magenta's private tutor too! Way-hey! Can't wait – just what I need; more things in common with the very person I'm trying to get out of my life. Not to mention the fact that I get straight As most of the time anyway. I mean, just how many qualifications does she think I need to be a DJ?

Still, Magnus is coming round to work on our track tonight and rehearsals for the actual concert start next week. I suppose that's something to look forward to.

3

Magenta

Have things started to look up in my life, or what? The first fantastic thing to happen to me is: I am now in the most brilliant girl band ever! And we're called Spangle Babes!

It turns out that I'd got the totally wrong end of the stick about the whole Battle of the Bands thing. Seema explained that when Hattie had said there were *four* of them in the band, she'd been referring to the four singers. I'd got a teensy bit teary about it at the time but, as she pointed out, we can't all be good at everything (although she can talk because she seems to be!) and singing just isn't my forte.

'You were always going to be in the line-up, Madge,' she explained, as she was eating her packed lunch and looking at this geeky boy at the next table. 'But we saw your role as more of a managerial post.'

'Managerial sounds good,' I said, warming to the idea. 'Yes, I can see myself as a manager.'

'And we thought you could design our costumes too,' Arlette said.

'I am excellent at fashion design,' I agreed.

'And you can help us with the choreography,' Seema suggested.

'Oooo! Choreography! I love dancing.' And then I had a brainwave. 'I know! I can be a backing dancer!'

Seema spun round – a bit too quickly, actually, because a crisp went the wrong way and she started choking. Arlette and I were patting her on the back till she finished coughing then she said, 'Well, actually, Madge, we were thinking that the four of us would do the dancing as we sang.'

'Yes but all the girl bands do that – think how original and unique it would be to have a separate backing dancer.'

'Well, I'm not sure.'

I was starting to feel a bit miffed to be honest, because although they'd said they wanted me in the band, it didn't look that way from where I was sitting. They weren't even taking my brilliant suggestion seriously.

'Trust me.' I was determined to convince them. 'It would be amazing. I can see it now; the four of you would be in coordinating clothes – maybe pale pink or something – with sparkles and everything, of course. And I'd be in a deep pink to complement you.'

'Erm . . .'

'Or silver, if you'd prefer.' I was on a roll. 'In fact, even better than a backing dancer – how about a *fronting* dancer? I could be at the front of the stage doing dance moves that illustrate the lyrics of the song. How brilliant would that be?'

'Well . . .' Arlette began.

'I can see it all now.' I was getting really excited. 'We could start in total darkness, right. And then, as the music starts, the lights could come up really slowly and the first thing would be me in—'

'To be honest, Madge, I'm not sure how that would work,' Seema interrupted. Honestly! She's got no imagination. I was starting to feel a teensy bit disappointed again, but then she obviously saw the genius of my idea and added, 'But it's definitely something to think about.'

'Excellent!'

'Although it'll have to be agreed with Hattie and Chelsea,' she went on.

'Of course.' Like that was going to be a problem!

But actually, it did prove to be a problem because Chelsea and Hattie were amazingly resistant to the idea of me being their fronting dancer. Between you and me, I think it was a bit of jealousy on their part. You know – they didn't want me stealing the limelight. They may be brainboxes, but emotionally, they're very immature. In the end I agreed to stay in the background – on condition that they let me mime the words so that it looked like I was as much one of the band as they were. And it's all sorted now; the band's been entered for the contest and I am officially a Spangle Babe! Wow! How show-biz does that sound?

The second amazing thing to happen is (and this really is so amazing you might get a head-rush just reading about it) I did brilliantly in my exams! OK – I know the term brilliantly is all relative and if Seema had got my grades her parents would probably have grounded her for life, but Seema is a total boffin so it's not fair to compare us.

Of course the downside of getting good results is that my dad has given all the credit to the Dung-beetle. 'You see, Magenta, didn't I tell you that Mr Dumbarton was a good teacher? And your results just go to prove it.'

Oh yeah – like he answered the questions for me, did he? I don't think so! And wouldn't you think that such hard work on my part would've earned me at least some time off for good behaviour? But oh no! All it means is that now Dad's even more determined to make me stick out my sentence and keep going to the geriatric human computer every single Saturday morning – for two hours! Two whole hours! That's like a quadruple detention every week. It is so unfair!

Last week that 'excellent teacher' (aka my revolting dung-beetle of a tutor) was slopping up and down his kitchen in these disgustingly old slippers with my essay in one hand and a mug of tea in the other. It was one of those mugs that says: *old teachers never die, they just lose their class*. Ho ho ho! Funneeee – not! Personally, I think he probably died a long time ago – either that or he's on borrowed time: he must be at least a hundred and ten.

He put his mug down on the draining board and gave me a look that could've melted metal. 'Did you do *any* research for this, Magenta?'

Personally, I think research is overrated, so I decided to tell a teensy little porkie because, after all, a lie isn't really a lie if it's:

a) what the other person wants to hear and

b) a way of saving your own life.

And this one qualified on both counts.

I put on my most hurt expression (so that he'd feel guilty about even questioning the amount of research I'd done) and said, 'Of course, Mr Dumbarton – lots.'

He's got these beady little laser-eyes that bore into you and make you feel about the size of an ant, and eyebrows that go right across his forehead like a caravan of caterpillars so that he looks like a demented dingbat.

'Then pray tell how you came to your opening sentence – and I quote – "*An Inspector Calls* is a police-drama written by a vicar."?'

Uh-oh! I'd left it till the Friday night before my lesson to write the essay and I'd forgotten to bring my book home so I'd rung Arlette to ask her what the play was about. The trouble was, we'd got on to talking about other, way more interesting, stuff – like the fact that Spud's having a party next weekend and:

1) She reckons Daniel fancies her (yeah, right – dream on, Arl!) and she's going to make a

move on him at the party. My gran always says: *What you don't hear; you must feel* – and sadly, I think Arlette's going to feel pretty stupid when she makes a total prat of herself in front of everyone.

2) Seema's thinking of binning Hayden West after more than a year together (I knew she'd been eyeing up that geek in the dining hall) and asking someone else to go to the party with her but she won't say who. I hate it when people you trust start keeping secrets!

3) Spud and Angus had a fight over who was going to ask Chelsea to the party – but,

4) Chelsea's going with Ben, Arl's ex! Which Arl doesn't mind because even when they were going out, she always had one eye on Daniel.

So, by the time I got off the phone, I'd completely forgotten what she'd said about the play. But at least I'd written something – although the Dung-beetle didn't seem to appreciate that fact at all.

He was rabbiting on, '. . . metaphysics . . .' OK – Arl didn't tell me it was a scientific play. I'd better have a word with her about that. '. . . social class system . . . yadda . . . yadda . . . yadda . . . J B

Priestley . . .' Of course – Priestley! I knew she'd said the guy who wrote it was something to do with religion! Let's face it: you hear Priestley; you think vicar. It was an easy enough mistake.

And, speaking of religion, the Dung-beetle seemed to take my F-grade essay as his cue for this week's sermon: 'You cannot rest on your laurels, you know, Magenta. You might have gained a C in your exams but you have a long, long way to go before you sit your GCSEs blah, blah, blah, blah, blah . . .' and on and on and on.

Why do teachers (and parents come to think of it – in fact most people who reach adulthood) do that – drone on about education and qualifications and jobs? They tell you to make the most of your life then go and make sure you do the exact opposite by sucking the joy out of everything.

Honestly, I really hate going to the Dung-beetle's and now, to make matters even worse, Daniel is going as well – and he's got the slot straight after me! So, even if I manage to avoid him all week at school, I can't help but bump into him every Saturday morning. Of course, I think it's all a ploy on his part to wheedle his way back into my life. Why else would a straight-A, brown-nose brainiac need to go to a private tutor? You see, ever since I dumped him, I've suspected that he still fancied me; I even told Arlette when she was going on about asking him out – but would she listen to me? Ooooooh no! This just goes to prove it, though. Well, he's in for a BIG disappointment because it's too late. I am so over him!

Which brings me to the third brilliant thing that has made my life do a total one-eighty-degree turn for the better – Spyros Evangelides! (Or Spyro, to his mates.) Ooooo – he is soooooooo spyrolicious!

I must admit, he's not my usual type at all; in fact, scarily enough, he bears more than a passing resemblance to Spud in the hair department – all flapping about like a mad mop. But, whereas Spud's hair is just plain greasy, Spyro's has that fantastic tousled look to it. And, of course, he's way more good-looking than Spud (which, sadly, applies to most people in our school).

We were at the first run-through for Battle of the Bands and the dhol drummers were just coming off stage. Jac Dhillon and Sundeep Deol were trying to trip each other up as they came down the steps and Ms Keyes was getting her tights in a twist as she faffed about with her clipboard like a decapitated hen.

'Come along, boys; when I said get off the stage quickly I didn't mean by ambulance. Now, who's next? Spiral Thrust – you ready?'

A group of mostly Year 11 boys went up on to the stage and started to plug their guitars into these huge amplifiers. One of them was the geeky guy Seema had been staring at in the dining room.

'See that boy on lead guitar?' she whispered in my ear. I didn't know a 'lead guitar' from a 'follow fiddle' but I nodded anyway. 'Well, he's in my music group and he's Grade 8 classical guitar. You should hear him play – he's amazing.'

'Wow?' It's hard to know what to say when Seema starts going on about her highbrow intellectual (i.e. boring) stuff.

'So, do you fancy him?' I was determined to suss out who it was she was going to take to the party.

'Not everything's about fancying people, you know, Madge. I just really admire his musical prowess.'

'Yes – I saw you admiring his musical prowess in the dining hall – remember?'

'Madge!' Seema slapped me on the arm. 'For one

thing I'm still going out with Hayden and for another, Gregory's . . . well, he's . . . anyway he's only in our year, you know,' she said, changing the subject, 'and Spyros Evangelides asked him to play with his band.'

She pointed across the hall to where Spyro was sprawled across two chairs looking soooooo cool. It was the first time I'd really noticed him around school. But when I saw him, it was like my legs turned to marshmallows.

'Oh my God, Seema! He is so gorgeous!'

Our hall has those chairs that link together in rows and Spyro was sitting sideways on one of them with a bandana round his head and his legs hanging over the arm so that his Converse baseball boots were on the seat of the next chair.

Seema screwed up her nose. 'You think?'

'Ya-ha!' It is such a good job we fancy different types. Can you imagine the rivalry if we both had the same tastes in boys?

'Spyros Evangelides!' Ms Keyes' voice was reaching such a level of panic that I'm surprised the sound equipment wasn't squeaking. 'On the stage please – we're waiting! And get your feet off the chair.' Then she added this lame little, 'Please.'

Spyro didn't move. 'No way! You can't seriously expect me to play on *that* drum kit?'

Ms Keyes looked as though she was about to burst into tears. 'Spyro, I have four weeks to get this event organised. The school equipment may not be the best in the world and at the actual concert you can bring in your own drum kit if you want, but this rehearsal is for me to see the approximate length of each act and the type of music you're going to play. Please just run through the song you're going to perform because I need to work out a varied running order for the competition.'

He gave this sort of huff and then slipped his legs off the chair – really slowly. He walked up the steps on to the stage and sat down on this little stool behind the drum kit. Wow! He was so cool – talk about commanding the stage! The rest of the band all waited till he sat down. Then he started tapping his drumsticks to count them in.

'One, two, three, four.'

And suddenly, he went from laid-back to electrifying in one strum of Greg the Geek's guitar. It was like Spyro'd been plugged into the National Grid. He started crashing and banging away and tossing his drumsticks in the air (and, even more importantly, catching them again). To be honest, I felt a bit sorry for the rest of the band because hardly anyone was paying any attention to them: Spyro was sooooooo amazing.

At one point he even took off his shirt, got up and stood with one foot on the stool and one on the drum at the side. Phwoar! Talk about Tarzan on Pepsi Max! I could hardly take my eyes off him for the whole rehearsal.

We were doing our run-through straight afterwards so Spangle Babes were going on to the stage as Spiral Thrust were coming off.

'Wow! You were amazing,' I said as he walked past me.

Spyro tossed one of his drumsticks into the air and caught it behind his back. 'I know,' he said – only not in a conceited way; just really mature and confident.

'Good luck,' Greg the Geek said as we went past him. You see, I bet it is him that Seema's going to take to Spud's party.

Anyway, our bit went OK. Chelsea got all shirty because she said I hadn't learned the words properly. Hmm! Now let me think – do I *need* to know the words if I'm only allowed to mime? I don't think so! I mean, who's going to notice – durr! OK, so there was a teensy bit of a problem when I got the verses in the wrong order; I thought we'd got to the last line and I did this spectacular flourish type star-shape that we were going to end with – the only problem was, the others still had a verse to go and were all crouching down. Which is why it would make so much more sense for me to sing along with them – then I'd know where they'd got to.

Of course Daniel was there with his band of merry losers; they're doing some lame electronic thing that sounds like a thousand rabid cats being pummelled to death with pneumatic drills. There aren't even any words to it! Apparently they made it up in Music Technology. How pathetic is that?

But, right at the end, I had a fourth reason to be pleased that my life was taking a turn for the better – Spud has invited everyone from the Battle of the Bands to his party! Every single person! That must be about fifty of us altogether. It's going to be the best party ever – and even better, his mum and dad are going to be away that weekend, so there won't be any boring adults to spoil it – not that I'm going to let Dad and Belinda know that.

And call me Mystic Madge but, from the way he was so cool coming off the stage, I got the distinct impression that there was sparkage between me and Spyro!

Ooooo – I can't wait for the party!

4
Spud

Way-hey! Is Magenta going to be able to resist me after my cunning plot to win her over? No chance! She'll be like putty in my palms by the time I've finished.

To be fair, I don't want to claim all the glory for myself – it was my sister, Kerry, who had the first brainwave. Which is pretty amazing because IQ isn't something you usually associate with my sister – unless IQ stands for *Issues Queen*! Because, let's face it, she's got those about pretty much everything (issues, that is) – although mainly about school; in fact she's hardly ever there, even though this is supposed to be her exam year!

But as soon as Mum and Dad told us that they were going to Great Auntie Gladys's diamond wedding in Didcot for the weekend, that dormant brain cell of hers started revving up and getting into gear. Of course, I was one step ahead of her initially, and I'd already made a mental note to have the lads over for the night. You know, get in a pizza, watch a few DVDs – the usual. It came as a shock when Kerry dragged me into the downstairs cloakroom – in fact, I thought for a minute she was going to put my head down the bog again, like she used to when we were little, so it was a relief when she just grabbed me by the collar of my school shirt and pushed me against the wall.

'Listen, nerd-knuckles . . .' The worst thing about being a younger brother is that older sisters have absolutely no respect for us younger – and, I might add, often wiser – siblings. '. . . I'm going to have a party once the olds are out of the way – OK?'

To start with, I wasn't really following her. 'OK – but do you really think they'll allow it?'

'Jeez! Where *were* you when they gave out brain cells? They won't have to *allow* it because they won't know about it.' She twisted my tie even tighter. 'Will they?'

'Of course not,' I gulped.

'Dipstick!' Kerry let go of me so that I could breathe again.

'Aw, wicked! A proper party without any parents . . .' I started, rubbing my neck to get the circulation going again.

'Whoa – hold it, zit-face!' She grabbed my shirt

again. 'I said *I* was having a party, not you. You can go and stay with one of your feeble little friends for the night.'

It was clear that she wasn't going to be reasonable, so I employed my superior intelligence. 'Awwww! No way. Please, Kerry. Just one or two mates, that's all. And we'll stay in my bedroom, I promise.' And then I went in for the kill. 'If you let me, I swear I won't tell Mum and Dad.'

And she agreed! You see what an evil genius I am?

So, Stage 1 of my brilliant plan to get Magenta back was hatched. I must admit, when Mum and Dad first told us they were leaving us alone, I'd erred on the side of caution and only thought of having the boys round, but as soon as my intellectually-challenged sister decided to open it up to all-comers, I realised that I could invite Magenta as well – plus a select group of her friends of course – so as not to make it too obvious; subtlety's always been my strong point.

Then Stage 2 began to formulate: I'd get her jealous! Oh yes! I was amazing myself. I started coming on to Chelsea Riordan and spreading the word round that I was going to make a move on her at the party. And people believed it – especially Angus. But to be fair, he's been holding a candle for Chelsea ever since the youth club trip to bowling last year – although come to think of it, he holds a candle to most things, so that's not saying much – boom, boom! Am I on fire, or what? Oh yes – and again! Get it? On fire: candle? Boy – I am razor sharp today! I'm thinking a career in stand-up is definitely the way forward for me.

Anyway, to get back to Operation Magenta – Stage 3 came to me in a moment of pure inspiration. We were at the first run-through for Battle of the Bands and Magenta and her lot kept looking over in my direction and smiling. I could see that they were impressed with our band, Luminance, and as Magenta's split up with Danno there wasn't any reason for her to be smiling at him, now was there? So the obvious conclusion was that she was making a play for yours truly. And at that point I was happy for her to think that I was a fully paid up part of the band. Unfortunately, once we got on stage, things went a bit pear-shaped and I took an executive decision to distance myself from the whole set-up.

Daniel and Magnus – our supposed front men – had been making this track in Music Technology, but there was some problem with the samples and then Danno went and totally cocked up the mixing. Not to put too fine a point on it – they were pants! And I say *they* advisedly – I mean, all Angus and I did was hump a few bits of equipment up on to the stage, so their crap performance had absolutely nothing to do with me.

To make matters worse, there's this prat called Spyro who thinks he's some sort of rock-god just because he can bash a few cymbals and make a lot of noise. He was grinning and taking the piss out of us as we came off stage so that everyone started laughing.

'Luminance? More like *Lame*-inance.'

'Never mind, boys,' Ms Keyes said. It didn't bother me, of course, but I think she could see that Danno was upset. 'It's only the first rehearsal. You've got time to sort it out.'

There was this sound like a horse with wind, which turned out to be Spyro again.

'How much time? They'll need to slip through a worm hole if they're going to get that sorted in four weeks.'

I was just going to floor him with some of my biting sarcasm when it came to me: I needed to use my enemy's strength against him. It's an old Kung Fu strategy I've learned from watching Jackie Chan and Bruce Lee films. Instead of trying to beat him at his own game, I could kill the jibes and win the popularity vote in one go. You see, that's where the skill of a ninja comes in handy.

'Party at my house next Saturday! You're all invited!' I shouted across the hall. 'Bring some crisps and something to drink.'

Boom chakka lakka! Suddenly, I was everyone's mate. Way to go or what?

On party day – or P-Day, as I like to refer to it – Danno was over at mine all day downloading tracks from the Internet to make a compilation album of all our favourite music. Kerry and her posse of poseurs were making fruit punch in the kitchen all afternoon instead of moving the furniture out, like I'd told her she ought to. Even worse, she'd used the inscribed crystal punch-bowl that Mum had won for being Cosmic Cosmetics' Rep of the Year last year. We'd hardly seen her all winter because she'd been out there selling more make-up door-to-door than anyone else in the whole of our area.

'Kerry!' I yelled at her. 'You can't use that. It's special.'

'So are you, but I use you all the time!' she laughed. And all her friends started laughing too – lucky for my sister that sticks and stones may break my bones but words can't touch a Dragon Master.

And then I went into the fridge to get Danno and myself a couple of cans of Coke but every shelf was like a massive red or green wobble board. When I looked closely, the whole thing was full of dozens and dozens of tiny individual jellies. So that explained why it'd taken them all afternoon to make a single bowl of fruit punch.

I said to her, 'Jelly? What's next – plastic bowls of iced gems? We're not little kids you know, Kerry! This is supposed to be our first grown-up party.'

She slammed the fridge shut. 'It *is* going to be a "*grown up*" party, which is why you and your freaky friends had better not touch any of this, right! These are for *my* mates and no one under Year 11 is allowed through that kitchen door tonight – understood?'

She is so juvenile. Like my friends would even want to have jelly at a party. We grew out of that when we were about six.

'Losers!' I said.

'Right back at you,' Kerry shouted after me as I left them to their infant food-fest.

In the end Danno and I lugged the dining chairs, the coffee table and the TV into the garage but we couldn't manage the settee or Dad's Barker-lounger. We just moved them to the edge of the room, rolled up the rug that usually goes in front of the gas fire and hid it between the settee and the radiator. We left the dining table in too so that people could put drinks and crisps on it, and then we were all set!

'See you later then, Spud,' Danno said when he went home to get changed.

'Cool – you'll be back about eight, right?' I asked. Not that I was nervous or anything, but I thought it would be good if he was there with me when people started arriving – you know, just for a bit of moral support. I mean this was going to be our first proper party so it was a sort of rite-of-passage and I thought it would be good to face it together – like men.

'I'll try.'

'Try? Hey, dude, let's have a bit of solidarity, here.' As I said, it wasn't that I was scared or anything but, when all my sister's crew started to arrive, the last thing I wanted was to be the only Year 10 in a sea of no-brain Year 11s.

'I'll do my best, OK?'

'Whoa, whoa, whoa! All you have to do is go home and get changed. What's the big deal? I mean it's not going to take you *that* long, is it?' He only lives round the corner.

He started running down the road. 'Don't worry. I'll be there as soon as I can.'

'You'd better!' And I went up to my room to prepare for Stage 4 of my cunning plan – dressing for impressing! I was thinking 'urban' was the way to go tonight – low batties and the hoody Nan and Granddad brought me back from NY. It is truly nang! Oh yes – Magenta was going to be mine again before the end of the night. Bring it on!

OK, so it wasn't Windows that made Bill Gates a billionaire – it was the nine thousand, nine hundred and ninety-nine other programs before it that didn't work. And the same thing seemed to be happening to me with Mission Madge. I was encountering a few technical hitches with my original plan – in fact, not just with Operation

Magenta, but with the whole party.

Problema nùmero uno – my brilliant 'getting off with Chelsea Riordan to get Magenta jealous' idea went straight into the snowball-in-hell category when Chels turned up holding hands with Ben Jestico. Bummer! But I don't give up that easily and lots of other girls had come on their own, so I'd just find someone else to pull in order to invoke a bit of the old green-eye.

Problema nùmero dos – Magenta arrived (looking as gorgeous as ever of course) arm in arm with Arlette Jackson – which you might think was a good sign because it meant she wasn't with a boy, but every time I tried to speak to her, they did a U-turn – her and Arlette linked together like they'd been superglued at the elbow.

Problema nùmero tres – my so-called mate, Danno, turned up an hour late – and wait for this – with Seema Karia! Talk about tossing a feline into a flock of pigeons! Now you might be wondering why this rates as a problemo, when it was probably doing me a favour in the Magenta stakes, but the real problemo wasn't Magenta and Dan – it was Magenta and Seema. Boy, did they go for each other big time! Magenta was screaming that Seema had betrayed her trust; Seema was yelling that she could go out with whoever she wanted and Magenta was a control freak. At least, that was the general gist of it – the music was so loud, it was hard to hear exactly. And then when they'd finished hurling insults at each other, they did this girlie hand-flapping thing, slapping each other on the arms like they were swimming doggy paddle out of water.

Which let to: major spanner in the proverbial – *Problema nùmero cuatro* – Kerry must have heard the commotion. She came out of the kitchen with one of Mum's cut-glass punch cups (the ones that normally hang off the rim of the punch bowl), full of fruit punch, and she only went and threw it over Magenta's head!

'AAAAAAAAGGGGGGHHHHH!' Magenta was standing with fruit punch dripping off her hair and all down her front. Actually, she looked well gorgeous. 'What the hell do you think you're doing? she screamed, picking up a bowl of crisps from the table and dumping it right over my sister's head.

Uh-oh – then things really started to kick off!

5
Magenta

As parties go, Spud's has to be the worst one EVER! In fact, I should think it was approaching an eight point four on the Richter Scale of social disasters.

The first warning shock came when Seema, my so-called best friend (OK – I know Arl's supposed to be my best friend, but Seema was definitely my second-best friend) went and turned up with Daniel! Don't get me wrong, she can go out with whoever she wants, but it was the sneaky way she went about it that got up my nose. Even before she dumped Hayden West, she was dropping hints about going to the party with someone else, but I never dreamed she could be so desperate as to go with slobber-chops, Daniel the Spaniel. And then she had the nerve to accuse *me* of trying to dictate who she can go out with! Yeah right – like I give a monkey's about her love life!

The second thing that really should have started my alarm bells ringing was that Kerry Pudmore, Spud's psycho-sister, only went and threw this disgustingly sticky liquid over my freshly-straightened and glossed hair that had taken me hours to do – OK, well, maybe not *hours*, but a pretty long time, anyway. Just because Seema and I were having a teensy little bit of a tiff about the way she'd betrayed me. Can you believe it? I was standing there in front of everyone with segments of mandarin orange plopping off my head and down my top. And even worse, Spud offered to eat them out of my hair for me – ewwww! Gross!

I was so mad at being humiliatingly half-drowned in punch (which, by the way, tasted distinctly weird and not like any fruit juice I'd ever tasted), plus being submerged under lumps of citrus, that I picked up this plastic pudding bowl of crisps from the dining table and plonked it down on Kerry's head. Ha! See how *she* liked haute coiffure à la snacks and nibbles!

And, just when I was standing there looking like a drowned fruit salad, Spyro Evangelides, the demon drummer himself, only went and walked in. This was so not how I'd hoped to impress him with my cool, sophisticated Spangle Babe image. Especially as he made this really dramatic entrance. He had a pink floral dress over the top of his jeans with a matching scarf tied round his head like a bandana and he was pirouetting in the doorway. He looked soooooo funny; really cute actually. Although, now I come to think of it, I'm sure I'd seen Mrs Pudmore wearing a very similar outfit on holiday last year.

'And here we have a fetching little pink number and coordinating head wrap, beautifully decorated with big red flowers and ideally suited to the modern man about town,' he said, giving a little twirl.

I must admit, he did look totally delish – in a Pirates of the Caribbeany-type way. Someone gave a wolf-whistle and Spyro flicked the back of his hair. We were all laughing – except Kerry and Spud.

'Take that off, you moron,' Kerry yelled at him.

Spyro put on this silly accent. 'Hey – she with crisp on head should watch who she call moron.' Then he looked over at me and this glint came into his eyes. (You see, I *knew* there was sparkage!) 'Excellent!' He nodded slowly and this smile spread across his face – right as he was looking at me! Ooooooo my tummy did back flips.

Although there's a slight chance that I might have misinterpreted him because the next thing he yelled was: 'Food fight!' And he lobbed the plate of jelly he was carrying straight at Kerry.

But Kerry was too quick for him. She ducked down and it hit Spud – full frontal!

'Aw man! This is my new hoody: all the way from the Big App—' But before he could finish, another jelly got him right between the eyes.

And suddenly it was a free-for-all. Kerry picked up a chocolate Swiss roll that someone had brought and hurled it at Spyro's head, but he managed to dodge it and instead it hit Shanti Wray right on her nose.

'You cow!' Shanti screamed and lobbed a Jaffa Cake at no one in particular. It caught Angus Lyle on the cheek so he hurled a muffin into the middle of the mass of people who were piling into the dining room using an Oriental rug as a shield.

Before you could say *Bun fight at the OK Corral*, food was flying everywhere: crisps and cakes, peanuts and jellies, zooming all over Spud's dining room. And when Mr and Mrs Pudmore's wedding photo took a can of Coke to the silver frame and smashed on to the floor, I knew it was time to duck and cover.

'Quick!' I grabbed Arlette's hand and we dived

under the dining table in a hail of Nobby's Nuts.

'Ow!' Seema got a chocolate chip cookie in the eye and my conscience got the better of me. I knew this was no time to let a stupid squabble over an ex-boyfriend get in the way of our friendship, so I reached up and pulled her down with us.

'Oh my God, Madge – now look what you've started,' Seema said, picking a chocolate chip out of her eyelashes.

'Excuse me?' I couldn't believe what I was hearing. Did I say *friendship*? Rewind! And anyway, look at her moaning about a stupid chocolate chip – I'd got half a fruit salad over me! '*I* didn't start it,' I said, indignantly. 'Kerry stupid-features Pudmore was the one who poured drink down me first.'

'Yes, but you could've been the bigger person and not retaliated,' Seema said, pulling a crumb along the length of her hair.

Honestly! I half expected her to morph into Mother Teresa any second. 'What is going on with you?' I asked her. 'First you keep these nasty little secrets about Daniel; then you try to land this on me. Have I done something to upset you, Seema?'

'Ohhhh for . . .' She stopped, took a deep breath, then carried on. 'Not everything is about you, you know, Madge!'

Whoa! Get her. She has definitely been spending way too much time with Daniel because, if I remember rightly, that's pretty much what he said to me when I dumped him at New Year. And I was just about to say, *hello – an original thought would be nice*, when Arlette suddenly burst into tears at the other side of me. I don't know if it was cabin fever setting in (OK so it might not have been the trenches, but sitting under the table did feel like a very confined space) but everyone around me was getting way too emotional.

'Stop it. Stop it, you two. I can't stand this. I want to go home,' Arlette wailed.

I looked at my watch. 'But Arl, it's not even ten o'clock,' I reasoned. 'We're allowed to stay out till eleven thirty. There's no way we can go home at this time: it's an abuse of privileges. If any one of us goes home early, the word will go round and the adults will think we don't need to stay out late and it'll ruin our social life – for ever.'

A paper plate of jelly squelched down on to the floor by my knee, so I edged back under the table and pressed myself against the double doors that led into Spud's garden.

'But this is horrible,' she cried, huddling up against me. 'Everything's getting messed up and my two best mates are fighting and . . . and . . . I'm scared of what my mum and dad will say if they ever find out about this.'

I must admit, she had a point about us fighting. And maybe Seema did too when she'd said I should've been the bigger person with Kerry. She was sitting near the front of the table with her chin on her hands and staring out at the chaos on the carpet. I crawled forwards and pulled her round to face me.

'I'm sorry for getting upset, OK?' See – I *could* be a bigger person.

'And I'm sorry for not being honest with you,' she said, putting her arms round me and giving me a big hug.

You see this is why it's so great to be a girl – we're so mature. Seema and I moved back against the French doors where Arlette was curled up looking as though she was under enemy fire.

I turned to Seema. 'If you want to go out with Daniel, you can. I don't mind – really,' I told her. 'Anyway, where is he?'

'But that's the point,' Seema said. 'We're not going out.'

'What!' Amazingly, Arlette's tears suddenly dried up!

'Just because we arrived at the same time, everyone assumed we were an item but we only met at the bottom of the road and walked the last bit together.'

It turns out it had all been a huge mix-up. She'd actually been on the phone to Geeky Gregory asking him to come to the party with her (you see – I *knew* she fancied more than his musical prowess) but – wait for this – he'd turned her down! Now that's a pretty hard blow to anyone's confidence – unless you're Spud, of course, who gets turned down all the time – but for Seema, it was massive. I don't think she's ever been turned down before, for anything – ever. As long as I've known her she's always been straight As, distinctions, leading lady, boy magnet etc., etc., etc. So rejection – especially from a geek like Gregory – really wiped her out. That's why she was late. She'd been getting herself together enough to come and face us, knowing that the guitar goon himself would be here too.

'I thought you said he wasn't your type?' I said.

She shrugged. 'He isn't really – but there's something about him. He's just really . . . nice. And we've got so much in common. I didn't want to say anything in case it all went pear-shaped – which it has done anyway.'

I put my arms round her. 'I am so sorry. Are you OK?'

Seema nodded. 'I'll get over it.'

'So that means Daniel's not taken?' Arlette was looking positively perky again.

Seema sighed. 'Well not by me, anyway.'

Arl rubbed her hands together. 'Excellent! Let's go and find him.'

Personally, I couldn't think of anything I'd rather do less than spend the rest of the party trying to fix my mate up with my ex, but compared to sitting under a table all night to avoid getting pelted with popcorn, it sounded relatively exciting.

I poked my head out from under the table and a barrage of Twiglets narrowly missed my eye, so I darted back again.

'I won't lie to you,' I said looking from Arl to Seema, 'it doesn't look good out there.' In fact, the whole room looked like a massive trifle.

'Why don't we go out through these French doors into the garden and then go back into the house through the kitchen? That way we can get into the front room where the music is.' One of my better ideas, I thought.

We undid the bolts at the bottom of each door and turned the key that was in the lock, then slowly pushed open the double doors. A blast of freezing air rushed us as we sneaked out from under the dining table into the garden. But, uh-oh:

'Wicked! Garden party!' a voice yelled.

And everyone from the food fight piled over the top of the table, out of the house and into the garden. Before you could say *Ground Force*, there were plants and clods of soil being lobbed everywhere – it was worse than indoors!

Keeping our heads down, Seema, Arl and I dodged a flurry of frozen compost and took cover behind the coal bunker before edging our way round the water butt and into the back door. The kitchen was amazingly empty of people – probably because they were all either in the dining room tossing food at each other or in the garden trashing the plants.

'Phew!' I said, taking a paper cup from the

worktop and scooping a ladleful of fruit punch into it. 'Let me grab a drink before we go and have a dance. I've had this stuff poured over my outside; I might as well sample it from the inside too.'

'I fancy one of these jellies,' Arlette said, picking up a red mini jelly and popping it into her mouth, whole.

But then: 'Ugggghhhhh!' we both said together, spitting out the jelly and the fruit punch at the same time.

'Eeeewwww! What *is* this?' I spat.

'Yuk! Gross!' Arl said, grabbing a piece of kitchen towel and wiping her mouth.

'Oh my God!' Seema exclaimed, pointing to the bin in the corner. 'No wonder all the Year 11s are off their heads.'

The top had come off the bin and there was a mountain of empty bottles piled up in it: vodka, gin, brandy – just about every sort of alcohol I'd ever heard of.

I was shocked. 'They haven't put them in the recycling box,' I said. 'How irresponsible is that?'

Seema looked at me and raised her eyes to the ceiling. 'I know your stepmother is the Queen of Green, Madge, but I think the irresponsibility goes way beyond not recycling the empty bottles.'

I looked from Seema to the bottles and back to Seema. Then I gasped. 'Nooooo! You don't mean . . .'

Seema shook her head in this *I-can-almost-hear-the-gears-clunking* type of way.

'Durrr! Of course that's what I mean. The punch and the jellies taste weird because they contain more alcohol than your average pub. We need to get out of here – fast.'

'Not before I've got rid of this stuff,' I said, picking up a tray of jellies and heading for the downstairs cloakroom. I'd seen Gran and Auntie Vee after one too many Baileys and, believe me, it wasn't a pretty sight.

'Leave it, Madge,' Seema said. 'If Kerry Pudmore and her lamebrain mates want to get tanked up and make prats of themselves, that's up to them. Let's just get out of here.'

'No way!' I was on a mission. 'Everyone's always harping on about doing good deeds, well this is my good deed to Spud's family – look at the state of this place, and it's all because of these. Arl, you take the punch and pour it down the sink, I'll pour this lot down the loo.'

Reluctantly, Seema grabbed another tray of

jellies and followed me, while Arl wrapped both arms round the punch bowl.

'Wow! This is amazingly heavy,' Arl said, picking up the crystal bowl and staggering across the floor towards the sink as waves of orange liquid slopped over the sides and on to the floor.

Just at that moment the back door opened and what looked like a small tree was speared across the kitchen. I dodged sideways as it hurtled past my left shoulder, allowing a couple of jellies to slide off my tray and splat on to the tiled floor.

'Whoops! Mind those jellies,' I warned Arlette. 'Don't slip on them.'

Seema and I took the trays into the hall towards the cloakroom while Arlette heaved the punch bowl on to the draining board and began pouring the punch away.

As I passed the door to the front room I could see a few people dancing and someone who looked suspiciously like Daniel lying on Mr Pudmore's Barker-lounger having a pretty passionate snogging session – although I couldn't make out who he was with. Chelsea and Ben were on the settee and Spyro, still dressed in Mrs P's dress and scarf (although now it wasn't so much pink and flowery as brown and flaky!), was in the middle of the room surrounded by pots and pans with a pair of wooden spoons. He was bashing away as though he was doing his drumming routine. I stopped to have a look but Seema rammed her tray into my back.

'Let's get a wriggle on, Madge, before anyone realises we're destroying this lot. Somehow I don't think they'll be too happy about it.'

Once in the toilet, we tipped the whole lot into the loo. Thank goodness there were only about twenty left, but even so, the whole bowl was full almost to the top of red and green slime – ugh!

'Good riddance!' I said, pushing the handle to flush them away. Only it didn't flush them away. In fact, Seema and I watched in horror as the water rose higher and higher up the pan of the toilet. 'Noooooo!' I screamed and tried to flush it again. But it kept rising.

'Do something,' Seema yelled. 'Stop it.'

So I tried to push some loo roll down there to soak up a bit of the excess, but it only made it overflow even more quickly. There was water and jellies and toilet paper pouring right over the top of the toilet and down on to the floor of Spud's downstairs cloakroom. The carpet was swimming in this gloopy red and green mess – and it just kept coming.

'Help! Help! The toilet's exploded!' I cried, running back towards the kitchen to get some towels to try and mop it up.

But just as I was passing the front room, who should come out holding hands with this little Year 9 girl called Jodi – but Daniel! (Cradle snatcher!) I ran smack into him.

'Owww!' I cried as we both fell in a heap in the middle of the hall.

'Done it!' Arlette called, turning round with the empty punch bowl, but when she saw Daniel and me sprawling about on the floor together, she burst into tears. 'How could you!' She turned to run away but her foot slipped on the jelly that I'd dropped earlier and, as her feet slithered in opposite directions across the tiles, the cut-glass punch bowl was propelled upwards into the air.

'Nooooooo!' I screamed, leaping to my feet and making a dive for it.

And guess what? I caught it! How sporty was that? Wow! I amaze myself sometimes. But, just as I was congratulating myself on saving the

Pudmores' family heirloom, the music suddenly died. And out of the silence:

'MAGENTA!' Uh-oh! It was my dad! And he was standing in the doorway of Spud's kitchen.

'Aaaaaggggggh!' I almost leapt out of my skin.

And, as I jolted at the shock of seeing Dad, the punch bowl leapt out of my hands and did a triple Salchow in the air. The next few seconds seemed to last an hour. I was frozen with horror; helpless to do anything except watch it glint in the light and send dozens of little sparkles across the kitchen as it spun upwards then plummeted down. (It was quite a pretty effect actually; a bit like a big glass glitter-ball.) But, would you believe it, the same bowl that I'd caught so easily when Arlette had dropped it, only went and slipped right through my hands without even touching them! Eeek! All I could do was stand there and watch as it smashed into a thousand pieces on the ceramic tiles. There was a deafening crash then, as everyone went into stunned silence, a sort of hissing noise as all the shards of glass scattered across the floor.

I caught Dad's eye and it was like staring into the face of a rampaging rhinoceros. There was nothing else for it; I was just going to have to do the decent thing.

'Ooops! Butter-fingers,' I said.

Uh-oh! The decent thing didn't have quite the effect I'd been hoping for.

6
Daniel

Mum's always saying: *Hindsight is a wonderful thing, Daniel.* But, to be honest, I hadn't really understood what she meant until Spud's party.

To start with everything had been great: Spud and I had made this brilliant compilation album off the Internet and I was in charge of the music in the front room; people had brought loads of food and Coke and stuff and, the closer it got to the kick-off, the better the idea of not having any parents lurking in the background seemed. (Which, by the way, is where the 20:20 rear-view vision comes in.)

Although, to be fair, for most of the evening, I had no idea what was happening in the rest of the house. It was only when I heard Magenta screaming something about an exploding toilet that I even ventured out of the front room. (I'd been way too preoccupied – if you catch my drift!)

And the reason for my preoccupation was this girl called Jodi Plock. She's the lead singer in an Emo band called Dead Petals and she'd been coming on to me big time at Battle of the Bands rehearsals. Even at the party she was all, 'I love the track you're doing for the concert, Daniel' and 'You're so talented, aren't you?' and 'Did you do the music for the party, Daniel? Wow, it's brilliant.' After a while I thought, *what the heck – I'm single again. Why not go for it?* So I did – until I heard Magenta yelling from the hall.

Now, I know Magenta is a tad prone to dramatising situations but, let's face it, she's also not exactly an accident-free zone. So when she sounded genuinely panicky about blowing up the toilet, it brought back memories of when Mum first went back to work when I was little. She'd hired this old lady called Dolly to help her with the housework. But it turns out that health and safety wasn't exactly Dolly's strong subject; she'd just finished cleaning the toilet and putting a load of loo cleaner down it when she'd decided to have her lunch – in the bathroom! She'd unwrapped her sandwiches and it seems that hygiene wasn't the only thing Dolly didn't grasp – her knowledge of chemistry was pants too – because she only went and tossed the tin foil into the toilet with the bleach! There was this massive chemical reaction that blasted the whole bog to bits.

So, even though Magenta and I aren't really speaking, I thought she must've done a Dolly. I grabbed Jodi's hand and ran out to find out what was going on. But it was only then that the true horror of what was happening in the rest of the house really hit me – although not before Magenta did. Wallop! I'd only just got to the hall when she barged into me like some sort of Tasmanian Devil and knocked me for six – face down in all this disgusting gunk.

'What the . . . ?' I yelled at her.

'Ohmygod! The toilet . . .' she blubbed.

But before she could tell me what had happened:

1. Arlette let out a whimper and started snotting for Britain by the sink.

2. Magenta jumped up, leapt into the kitchen and did a dive-catch worthy of the England square leg. It was pretty impressive, I must say. Magenta's never been known for her sporting ability, but it just goes to show what you can do with an adrenaline boost.

3. Curtis appeared out of nowhere, yanked the plug out of the socket so that the sound system went down and started screaming at

Magenta. And boy, when I say screaming, I mean cover-your-ears, board-up-the-windows and head-for-the-nearest-fallout-shelter screaming!

At the time, I couldn't work out why on earth he would want to turn up at Spud's – especially as Magenta had come clean about going over there. Although, like the rest of us, she had omitted the tiny details of the party and the lack of adult supervision. But that should've meant that he had just enough info to allay any parental suspicion, shouldn't it? So, naturally, I was thinking that someone must have grassed us up.

But it seems not. It was one of those bloke/baby press-the-panic-button scenarios. Belinda had been having stomachache all evening – which, according to Mum, was just her body practising having contractions. To be honest, I switched off when she was explaining – way too much information! All that baby stuff is best left to the women if you ask me. But Mum was on a bit of a high about it – seemed to think it was exciting. I suppose being a nurse she has a different definition of 'exciting'. To me, 'exciting' is me and Lewis Hamilton, neck and neck up to the finishing line at Silverstone;

having babies is only one step up from an in-growing toenail.

But Curtis, poor bloke, had been tearing his hair out – not that he's got much left to tear! Florence and Venice have gone to Jamaica (Florence reckoned she needed a rest so that she'd be fully fit to help when the baby's born); Magenta was out at Spud's; Mum and Donald were at the theatre and the midwife was on another delivery. In the end he couldn't take it any more and he'd panicked. He'd practically frogmarched Belinda to the car, insisting that she went to hospital, and then driven straight round to Spud's to pick up Magenta on the way.

Ironically, by the time he'd kicked everyone out of the house and given Spud, Kerry, Magenta and me an earbashing, Belinda's pains had stopped, so they went straight home again. Although not before he'd organised a massive clear-up operation for the next day before Sheila and Malcolm got back from Didcot.

About a dozen of us had turned up; mainly Spud's friends – of course! Kerry and her bubble-brain mate, Shanti, had staggered downstairs at about lunch time, then gone straight back to bed again – despite Curtis's Raging Bull impersonation!

If it hadn't meant dumping Spud right in it, I'd have been tempted to leave the mess and let the airheads take the punishment they deserved. As it was, it was down to the ones who hadn't even trashed the place to clear it up – which sucks by anyone's standards!

We'd got round to Spud's at nine in the morning and had been working like idiots (under the supervision of Commandant Curtis Hawk-Eye) to get it all done by the ETA of two o'clock. In the end, I thought we'd done a pretty good job – although there were one or two casualties:

1) Roughly ten per cent of Sheila's clothes have had to be binned and the rest will probably need some sort of industrial solvent if they're ever going to be worn again.

2) Malcolm's prize Japanese bonsai tree had found its way into the chest freezer and was sandwiched between the petits pois and the Mungo Cherry ice cream.

3) Despite Curtis's best efforts with the superglue, Sheila's punch bowl is a lost cause.

4) As soon as Jodi and I had vacated Malcolm's Barker-lounger, Spyros Evangelides had

leapt on it and tried out his stand-up drumming routine on the chandelier. In the cold light of day, the chair was now a three-piece suite in its own right with the seat, the back and one of the arms in separate rooms.

And:

5) As a result of Spyro's drumming, several crystal droplets from the chandelier had ended up in the tropical fish tank.

But apart from that, by the time we'd finished, everything was pretty much as Spud's mum and dad had left it – if not better. Curtis had even hired a carpet cleaner so some things were even an improvement! Wouldn't you think, considering we hadn't even done (most of) the crime, that would've counted as doing the time? But, oh no!

That afternoon, Magnus was round at my house, working on our track for the Battle of the Bands.

'So where was the delectable Jodi Plock this morning?' he asked.

'Dunno,' I said, staring at the screen of my computer. 'Listen, what do you think about fading out the drum loop at bar thirty-six?'

'You are one jammy dodger, you know, Danno. She is hot, man!' Magnus was clearly more interested in who I'd pulled at the party than the fact that we had three weeks to the concert and, so far, we didn't have a piece that was worth performing.

'Yeah, she's OK.' I turned round to the keyboard that was wired up to my sound module and PC and began tapping two keys rhythmically. 'Then we could build up the tempo – really slowly, like this.'

'You gonna see her again?'

He was lying on my futon and I turned to stare at him. 'Are we going to do this track or not?'

'Wooooooo! Look who's getting his pants in a pickle!'

The truth is, Magnus was really starting to piss me off going on about Jodi. Don't get me wrong, she's really cute and pretty and everything – there's just something that doesn't quite feel right. I can't put my finger on it. I know she's a year younger than I am, but I don't think that's the problem because, let's face it, Magenta's almost a year younger than me and, most of the time we were going out, it was brilliant. Although, when I think about it, it was the maturity thing that broke us up in the end.

Anyway, Jodi's nothing like Magenta. She's

really funky and out there. Although maybe that's it; maybe she's a bit *too* out there. I mean, that was what was so great about going out with Magenta – we'd grown up together, so we had similar taste in most things – whereas Jodi's different: she's really off the hook. And, let's face it, Magenta's preferred way of dealing with feelings is to deny having any, but Jodi is so in touch with her emotions that it can be positively scary at times. Not that I'm comparing them, because that wouldn't be fair.

It wasn't that Jodi was a bad kisser either. In fact, she's pretty good – easily as good as Magenta. It's just that, when our lips met, there wasn't that electrical charge shooting through me that I expected there would be. In fact, if I'm being honest, it was a bit of a disappointment. When Magenta and I used to kiss, it was like Bonfire Night and New Year and Diwali all rolled into one going off in my stomach. It was amazing. But with Jodi – nothing! Although, as I said, I'm not going to get into comparisons.

I turned to Magnus. 'What do you think?' I highlighted the riff on the computer and let it play. But we both screwed up our noses. A bit like Jodi, it wasn't quite right.

'Neh! It's not working; it needs something else.' Magnus was lying with his ear pressed against the wall and I was getting the impression that his mind wasn't really focused. 'Hey, did you know you could hear Magenta through here?'

'Durr! How long have I lived here? Of course I know. What d'you think about a trumpet?' I tapped out the tune on the keyboard.

'Ssssh!' Magnus flapped his hand for me to fade out the music. 'Sounds like she's having a row with her old man.'

'So what's new? Magenta's always having rows with her old man.'

'Whoa!' He sat up and moved nearer to my pillow so that he could get even closer. 'Magenta's dad's only threatening to go to the school and tell them about Spud's party . . . He says the Battle of the Bands should be cancelled . . . because of anti-social behaviour!'

I shook my head to try and reassure Magnus. 'Listen, Curtis is an OK bloke but sometimes he overreacts. He's all hot air. It won't come to that.'

'It has come to my attention that on Saturday evening . . .' Old Crusher, our head teacher, was pacing up and down the stage in the hall with his hands behind his back, tapping one hand on the other and staring at his highly-polished shoes. He looked like Father Christmas on misery pills. He'd called together everyone who was taking part in the Battle of the Bands, plus Kerry Pudmore – and I was getting the distinct impression that it wasn't to congratulate us. '. . . the students assembled here . . .' He swivelled round and scanned us with his beady little eyes. '. . . perpetrated an act of grrrr-oss vandalism.' And he rolled his Rs to give it more emphasis.

Magnus kicked my leg and whispered, 'I thought you said Magenta's dad was an OK bloke who was all hot air? Sounds more like methane than hot air to me.'

It was true, I might have to rethink my assessment of Curtis.

I'm sure The Crusher had been watching too many Bond villains, because he was walking with very deliberate steps across the wooden stage and speaking in this voice that was so soft it was positively menacing. He was using phrases like 'breach of trust' and 'irresponsible' and 'bringing the school into disrepute'. Finally, he dropped his voice even lower, till he might as well have been delivering the death sentence. 'I am v-eeeeeery disappointed.' And, call me paranoid, but I'm sure he was looking at me when he said that. Then finally, the verdict that Magnus and I had been dreading: '. . . for that reason, I am cancelling the Battle of the Bands.'

So that was it. No more Battle of the Bands. No more £100 prize money. No more dreams of stardom. As we filed out of the hall, the atmosphere was so heavy, you'd have needed an industrial chainsaw to cut it. No one spoke – except for Kerry Pudmore, who seemed to think the whole thing was one big joke. Even Spyro 'Super Ego' Evangelides just loped out quietly with his head down. And too right. It was mainly down to him and his boozy bozos that the whole party had got out of hand.

'I'm so sorry, mate.' At least Spud had the decency to apologise.

I slapped him on the back. 'No worries, mate. Wasn't your fault.'

There was a tug at my sleeve.

It was Jodi. 'Hey, Daniel. Listen, I've had an idea.'

I looked at her. Her hair was tied up in ribbons at one side of her head and a couple of little plaits were sticking out randomly. She had these enormous earrings – way bigger than the school rules allow – and black nail varnish, which was definitely against uniform regulations. I could see why Magnus thought she was hot. For someone who normally had that 'pale and interesting' look, her face was distinctly bright and perky – in fact, she didn't look like all her dreams had just been shattered into a million pieces at all.

'Not now, Jodi. OK?'

Spud, Magnus and I walked off down the corridor in silence.

'It's OK to be upset, you know,' she called after me. 'I'll phone you later and we can talk!'

'OK,' I called back.

EeeeK! What was I doing? I'd been involved with girls I wasn't really into before and it never works out well – for anyone. There was this little voice in my head saying: *you know you ought to end it now, before it's even started*. But there was this other voice saying: *stop being such a wuss! She's cool, she's funky and she's up for it. What's your problem?*

Oh God! Why does life have to be so difficult?

7
Magenta

Do you want the good news or the bad?

OK, well, the bad news is that the Battle of the Bands has only gone and been cancelled! My dad – über snake in the grass that he is – only went and told The Crusher about Spud's party and now he's gone and cancelled the whole thing. So I'm not speaking to:

1) Dad – I cannot believe that I'm related to him – maybe I was swapped at birth and somewhere there's this really cool family with a fascist daughter who doesn't fit in?

2) Belinda – who, let's face it, could've stopped him if she'd wanted but she's so wrapped up in this baby stuff at the moment that she couldn't be bothered. Of course if Gran was here, she'd have brought him to his senses but she's cleared off on some nostalgia-fest with Auntie Venice. You see, eventually, they all catch the selfish gene when they've been around Dad for long enough.

3) The Crusher – not that we were exactly on speaking terms in the first place, but if we were, I'd definitely not be speaking to him now.

But the good news is – I've got a boyfriend. Well – ish! The 'ish' is referring to the good news, not the boyfriend, although, come to think of it – I'm not sure if he is a proper boyfriend, so it might also refer to the boyfriend bit too.

Anyway, the reason it's good news-ish, is that it's Greg the Guitar Geek! Can you believe it? Someone who turned down Seema actually asked *me* out! How much of a boost to my self-esteem is that? Of course the problem is that I'm not sure if I even like him that much, but that doesn't matter because – he preferred me to Seema!

And, even better, he's in Spiral Thrust, so that means that he'll tell Spyro that he's going out with me and Spyro will see me in a different light and realise that I can be a rock chick and he'll get jealous and ask me out.

Although, (I'm starting to think that I haven't thought this through properly) if the Battle of the Bands has been cancelled, there won't be any more Spiral Thrust – or Spangle Babes, come to think of it!

And there won't be any more rehearsals for me to try to impress Spyro. Oh no! If that's the case, I'll be going out with Gregory for nothing. And he's not even taking me anywhere nice – we're supposed to be going to a (boring) guitar recital at the (boring) Arts Centre. I'd better do something – and fast!

As Gregory had turned Seema down, I thought it was probably best not to tell her about my dilemma of not really wanting to go out with him. You see, I am sensitive (despite what some people might say about me) and that's what makes me such a good and loyal friend. Instead, I took the opportunity while Seema was at the lunch-time music club to run through my options with Arl.

'So, I can either wait till Saturday afternoon and then ring Greg and tell him that Belinda's gone into labour and I won't be able to go out with him . . .' I began.

But Arlette was in one of her unsupportive moods again. 'I'm not being funny, Madge, but at this rate, Belinda's going to go into the *Guinness Book of Records* as having had the most labours in one pregnancy.'

'Well, they're not all real,' I pointed out – fairly obviously, I thought.

Arl gave me one of her looks. 'That's my point.'

'You've lost me,' I said, gazing over into the corner of the quad where Spyro and his mates were playing air guitar.

'Haven't you ever heard the story of the boy who cried wolf?' I told you she was being unsupportive.

'Isn't he the one who wore the sheep's clothing?' I was getting impatient – what have wolves got to do with anything, anyway?

Arl shook her head, like it was *me* who was being stupid. 'Why don't you just tell Greg the truth – that he's not your type?'

'Well, yes,' I agreed. 'That is an option.' And then I had a brainwave. 'Or . . .'

Arl groaned.

'We could rearrange the Battle of the Bands!' I turned to Arl and took her by the shoulders. 'How brilliant would that be if we could get the contest reinstated and then there'd be rehearsals again and Spyro would see me as the saviour of the competition and he'd be really grateful . . .' Oh wow! I know I've said it before, but am I a genius or what?

Of course Arlette had to put the dampeners on my brilliant idea. 'How exactly are you going to do that? You heard The Crusher.'

'Leave it to me,' I said. 'No problem.'

Ten minutes later I was standing outside The Crusher's room – and not because I was on detention – which, if I'm not mistaken, is probably a first! Now, I know I'd said I wasn't speaking to him, but I decided that this was an exceptional circumstance. I'd thought about what I was going to say and opted to go with the argument that Belinda had used on Dad when he'd first said he was going to phone the school and dob us in. Actually, I'd been sent to my room at the time, but I could still hear them rowing from upstairs. Honestly, Belinda says it's important that the baby develops in a loving and stress-free environment but let's face it, you don't need a degree in genetics to work out that if you want a peace-loving hippy for a child, you don't choose some suburban Genghis Khan like my dad for the father!

Anyway, when The Crusher came to the door I opened my eyes really wide to look my most appealing as I delivered my speech.

'. . . so you see, sir,' I concluded, 'it wasn't the Battle of the Bands people who caused the anti-social behaviour at the party; it was the other disruptive element in Year 11 who don't have anything constructive to do with their time. And if the contest is scrapped and there are no more rehearsals, that'll mean more of us out there causing problems in the community because we've got no way of channelling all that teenage energy. It's not fair to punish people by taking away positive activities; you should impose sanctions instead.'

But it was clear that I was having about as much impact on The Crusher as Belinda had had on Dad.

'I am correct in thinking that you did attend the party, Magenta?'

'Yes, sir.'

'And were you aware that there were no adults present?'

'Yes, sir.'

'And did you attempt either to leave the party or to call an adult for supervision?'

Durr! What sort of a ridiculous question was that? 'No, sir.'

'Then I rest my case. My decision is final. Now go away and leave me to have my lunch in peace.' And he shut the door on me! How rude was that?

But I wasn't going to give up – there had to be a way of getting the Battle of the Bands on again.

That night, I was in my room *not* watching television – mainly because my dinosaur of a father won't allow me to have one of my own. But I'd gone upstairs as a matter of principle because I knew Dad wanted me to stay down and watch TV with him and Belinda. My dad's always going on about doing things as a family, so I thought: *right, then – I'll go and sit upstairs on my own. That'll show him!*

After The Crusher had been so rude to me, I'd gone back out into the quad and Greg had come over and given me this CD to listen to. It was by the (boring) guy we were supposed to be going to see on Saturday at the (boring) Arts Centre.

'He's being hailed as the new Segovia,' Gregory had said, handing me what I thought was a CD-Rom.

Personally, I didn't know what he was talking about. 'Thanks, but I'm not really into cars,' I'd replied.

Greg had laughed. 'Oh, you're so funny, Magenta – "drive the new Segovia – nought to sixty in three chords"!'

I laughed with him – I hadn't a clue what was so funny – but I thought, if Spyro was watching, it would look good if he thought I was enjoying myself with someone instead of just mooching around looking for a life.

Anyway, in my room that night, with nothing to do – except homework of course, but that's always a last resort – I decided to listen to the CD. And, as I suspected, it was more like something Dad would listen to, not someone of our age. I mean, it was all unplugged for a start, and there was no singing of any sort – at all! I was skipping through the tracks trying to find at least one with a catchy chorus so that I could sing to Greg and prove that I'd listened to it, when there was a knock on my French windows. I was a bit spooked to start with, because it was over a month since Daniel had been round to speak to me.

'Who is it?' I called.

'Who do you think it is: the tooth fairy?' he replied – unnecessarily sarcastically, I thought.

I drew back the curtains and he was standing on the balcony, shivering. 'Can I come in?'

I was going to say something back and then I remembered what Seema had said about being the bigger person, so I just opened the door and let him in.

He looked round and nodded. 'It's looking nice in here,' he said. 'I'd almost forgotten what it was like.'

OK, enough of being the bigger person. 'Daniel, it's only been four weeks – although, granted, it's taken me all that time to detoxify it and restore it to its former glory after you managed to trash it with all your boy stuff.'

Daniel walked back towards the window with his hands in the get-out-of-my-face position. 'Fine, you want to be like that, go ahead. I only came round so that you'd be the first to know that the Battle of the Bands is back on.'

What! 'No, wait.' Back to the bigger person plan. 'I'm sorry.' See: easy peasy lemon squeezy.

Daniel hesitated, as though debating with himself whether to accept my apology, then sat down on the edge of my bed. 'It's true; I've just had a call.'

'How? Who? I mean, what happened?'

'Whoa! Slow down.' Daniel started laughing. 'By the way, cool music.'

'Really?' I said, turning it down. 'Anyway, come on, tell me.' I sat down next to him and it was almost like old times – I mean old, *old* times; the good times, before we started going out, when we were mates and could laugh and joke together. 'Who rang? And why did they ring you first?'

'It was Jodi . . .' he began.

'Jodi! That little Goth girl from Year 9 that you were practically devouring at Spud's party?' OK – it's official – the bigger person stuff just doesn't work. 'What's *she* got to do with it?'

How could Jodi Plock with her shrunken T-shirts and coffin make-up possibly have got round The Crusher when I couldn't? What had she got that I hadn't? And, at the risk of labouring my point, she is only Year 9!

Daniel stood up. 'For your information, Magenta, Jodi is an Emo, not a Goth – there is a difference you know.' Yeah, right! 'And, as it happens, her uncle is Bruno at the Youth Centre. She's arranged for the contest to be held there instead of at the school. But, don't worry . . .' he opened the French windows and stepped outside, '. . . I won't be polluting your pretty pink palace with my boy stuff any more!'

And he disappeared back to his own room.

But not before I'd had the last word. 'Don't worry – you won't get the chance!' I retorted. Ha!

So the whole good news/bad news thing has done a total rewind and the good news is now that Battle of the Bands is on again – yay! But the bad news is that, as part of my plan to make Spyro jealous, I have to go to the (boring) guitar recital at the (boring) Arts Centre with my new (boring) boyfriend – boo!

By the time Saturday came, just to make my life a zillion times worse, Bruno had said that we could use the Youth Centre on Saturday mornings for rehearsals, but of course Mussolini downstairs has decreed that I have to go to the Dung-beetle's instead, which is so unfair! I mean, how am I ever going to get the dance moves and mime the words properly if I'm never there to rehearse? And then there was another problem – my clothing crisis. I don't mean that in the Oxfam-y kind of way, but what on earth do you wear to a guitar recital at an Arts Centre? In desperation, I phoned Seema.

'Just jeans and a top will be fine,' she said.

'Yes, but what sort of jeans? Crop jeans? Embroidered jeans? Skinny jeans? Boot cut? And what type of top?'

'Whatever – it really doesn't matter.' She

sounded a teensy bit peed off, if you ask me.

'Well it matters to me,' I told her.

'Look, Madge, the people there will have gone for the sole purpose of hearing the artist. No one will be interested in what you're wearing. You could go in a bin liner with a tulip up your nose and no one would care.'

Cheek! And then I realised what she was doing. 'If this is sour grapes because Gregory's taking me and not you . . .'

'Oh for . . .' Then she stopped. 'Actually, you're right. I'm sorry, Madge, I was being ridiculously childish. Don't forget it's an *Arts* Centre, so all the people will be really arty-farty types. You need to dress in arty clothes if you don't want to stick out like a sore thumb.'

See, I knew she'd wanted me to turn up in something frumpy just so that Greg would think he'd made a mistake and ask her out instead. Well, she couldn't pull the wool over my eyes!

'Arty?' Belinda's an Art teacher – you can't get much artier than that, now can you? 'You mean like Belinda wears?'

'Absolutely!' she said.

So, problem solved – before Belinda got

pregnant, she wasn't much bigger than me – which meant that I had the whole of her wardrobe to choose from. I spent the rest of the afternoon rummaging in her room till I found the most arty outfit I could. It was a pair of dungarees made of purple velvet with gold flowers embroidered all over – only they weren't your normal bib-and-brace type dungarees, they were like a grown-up version of the type babies wear – all baggy in the middle and gathered in at the ankles. I don't know who would wear anything like that outside a nursery – except maybe at a festival. But they were definitely arty. I then chose a hand-crocheted rainbow-striped jumper to wear under the dungarees.

'Oh my goodness,' Belinda said when I came downstairs and showed her. 'I haven't seen those since I was a student.' Which figures – arty types are always about ten years out of date.

Gregory was picking me up and he was clearly blown away by my attention to arty-farty detail when I opened the door to him.

'Wow! You look . . . er . . . colourful,' he said, taking a step back.

'Thank you, so do . . .' I looked at his grey cords and sweater. 'Anyway, let's go.'

'In public?' he said, looking up and down the road as though he was checking to see if anyone had seen him. 'I mean, *on* public transport?'

'Unless you've got a better suggestion.' What was the alternative – a magic carpet?

'It's just that it's a bit chilly out here – any chance your parents could drop us off?' he asked.

Honestly, what a wimp. But at least we saved the bus fare by getting a lift with Belinda.

The Arts Centre was in an old church. There were rows of seating like a cinema with a bar at the side and a stage at one end that had a high stool in the middle. At least Greg knew how to treat a girl on a date and offered to buy me a drink – not like some boys I've been out with who expected me to buy my own – cheek! I know I'm all for equality, but first dates are an exception – everyone knows that!

I looked at the rows of bottles behind the bar. What on earth should I order? I mean, it would look really immature just to have a can of Coke. I looked round to see what everyone else was drinking. Actually, it was the first time I'd noticed the other people and I must say, I wasn't impressed with all the arty-farty clothes that Seema had told me about.

In fact, when I looked closely, most people were in jeans and jumpers; I was definitely the most arty person there. And I could tell people were impressed because they kept giving me admiring looks. I made a mental note to text her and tell her how grateful I was for her advice.

While we were waiting by the bar, a guy came up and ordered a rum and blackcurrant. Not that I was remotely interested in the rum, but the blackcurrant sounded good.

'I'll have a blackcurrant juice please,' I told Greg. 'With lemonade.' How sophisticated was I – wearing arty-farty clothes in an Arts Centre and drinking blackcurrant and lemonade?

Gregory led us up to the back row and I sat down next to this woman who makes Auntie Heather look like Lady Laugh-a-lot. Honestly! Talk about having a face like an upset stomach! And you should've seen what she was wearing – she was a totally colour-free zone; white hair, white jumper and white trousers. Nothing arty-farty there – in fact, I must be honest, I was a teensy bit disappointed in the clientele at this place and I sent Seema a text to tell her – and also to thank her for the advice and let her know how things were going of course.

The lights went down and this guy came on and sat on the stool. Everyone clapped and he started to pluck away at the strings. Then *bring-bring* – Seema had replied to my text.

'Ssssh!' Mrs Bleach next to me hissed. 'Turn that thing off!'

So-orree! I turned the volume down instead and texted Seema back – I had to have some way of passing the time.

The guy on the guitar was twiddling away on his strings and Gregory was so enthralled, if I'd morphed into a purple porcupine next to him, I don't think he'd have noticed. My phone vibrated with another incoming message.

Then Domestos Woman nudged me again. 'I said, turn it off. Or I'll call for security.'

Humph! Honestly, some people would suck the fun out of anything. I turned off my phone, pushed it into the big patch pocket on the front of the dungarees and took another sip of my drink. This was even more boring than I'd thought it would be. I slid down in my seat and began to run through our dance routine in my head. If Dad wouldn't let me go to rehearsals, I had to find some way of practising – and Belinda's always saying that if you visualise something you can achieve it. I closed my eyes and pictured me in my pink outfit at the front of the stage. Step, step, step side; step, step, step, back; turn ...

...I was being handed a massive cheque for being the lead singer in the winning band, Spangle Babes. Everyone was cheering. Spyro was smiling at me. He was leaping over his drums to come to me ... when suddenly, from somewhere outside my dream, there was this twing, twang, twong noise and then a sharp stab in my ribs.

'TURN THAT RUBBISH OFF!' I yelled, waking up with a jolt. But as I woke up, my glass of blackcurrant tipped sideways and splashed on to Mrs Wash-out's white trousers.

'Oh for goodness' sake! You stupid girl! Now look what you've done!' She leapt to her feet and began dabbing herself with a tissue. There were big purple stains from her bosom to her knee. Ooops! 'This is very expensive Irish linen.' She looked me up and down. 'Not some jumble-sale fancy-dress costume.'

Cheek!

The guy on the stage had stopped playing and people were turning round and shushing.

'It's not my fault,' I pointed out to the man in front of me. 'She started it – she poked me in the ribs.'

'You were snoring!' Mrs Whiter-than-white argued. Then she called out, 'Security! Security!'

Two old men in cardigans came marching up the central aisle towards me. They looked more like Grandpa Joe than security officers, although, to be perfectly honest, they looked a lot less friendly than Grandpa Joe.

'Come with us, please, miss.'

At last! A chance to leave – phew! I grabbed my bag and started to follow them.

'Come on, Greg,' I said.

But would you believe it? He only stayed put! 'No way – I've waited ages for these tickets.'

How selfish is that? Did I say that he knew how to treat a girl? Well, you can cross that bit out! 'You are so dumped!' I said as I was being escorted down the aisle.

But guess what? He just shrugged! How mean is he? Seema had a very lucky escape if you ask me and as soon as I got outside I turned on my phone to tell her – but the battery had gone flat. Great!

So there I was standing outside on a freezing

February night looking like an escapee from a playpen when who should walk past but Kerry Pudmore and Shanti Wray with a load of boys who don't even go to our school.

'Oh look – Magenta's finally decided to dress her age!' Kerry called across the road. And they all laughed. Ggggrrr!

So now it'll be all round school and Spyro will hear about it and he'll think I'm some freak in weird clothing who can't even keep Geeky Greg as a boyfriend. What hope have I got of ever going out with him?

8
Arlette

It's only two weeks to the Battle of the Bands and I can hardly wait! Of course poor Magenta's upset because her dad won't let her go to the rehearsals on Saturday mornings. And I can understand that she probably feels left out and wants to be part of the whole build-up, but quite honestly, it's not like she's a major part of Spangle Babes or anything. In fact, and I know this might sound really horrible, but the rehearsals go way more smoothly when she's not there. And she's doing a fantastic job with the costumes and choreography – although maybe not so much the choreography, because we've changed most of the moves that she'd worked out initially because they were so complicated. We spent half our time trying to remember where our feet were going so we forgot the words and when we did remember them the routines were so tiring we were too out of breath to sing. But the outfits she's designed look great!

Her stepmum used to be our Art teacher but

she's on maternity leave at the moment, so she's helping Madge with our costumes. Between you and me, I think she's doing most of the sewing – I mean, I know Magenta is taking Textiles, but her strength is definitely on the design side rather than the actual needlework – not that I'd ever say that to her face.

Anyway, we're all going to be in silver and blue, which wasn't actually what any of us had wanted as a first choice. Hattie and Chelsea wanted us all to be in black and Seema's idea was silver. To be honest, I didn't mind what colour we wore, but I could understand why Chelsea and Hattie nearly had a cow when Madge came up with her usual suggestion. Anyone who knows them could see that pink just is not their colour, although it was a fact that seemed to have eluded Madge.

She'd spread out some fabric samples on the floor of Seema's bedroom where we were having our meeting. They spanned every tone from light rose to cerise.

'No way!' Chelsea had her hands on her hips. 'I told you – I am not wearing pink!'

'I'm not talking the really pale, baby shades . . .' Magenta said as she slipped the two palest fabric samples back into her bag. 'I know you'd look all washed out in those.'

'Cheers!' Chelsea said, giving her a look that could've floored an elephant at twenty paces. 'I don't actually care what shade of pink you're talking about, I am not wearing it!'

'With your colouring, you need something bolder. How about fuchsia?' Madge suggested, taking the piece of material that was the deepest pink and waving it in front of Chelsea's cheek.

'What part of "no" do you not understand?' I could see that Chelsea was getting pretty peed off.

'Actually, I'm with Chels on this one,' Hattie said. 'I'm not really a pink person either.'

Uh-oh! I was starting to feel distinctly uncomfortable. We'd chosen Seema's house for the meeting because she'd got the biggest bedroom, but it was beginning to feel very claustrophobic in there with all the tension.

'Arl?' Magenta turned to me. I knew she wanted me to support her argument. 'What do you think?'

Oh boy! You know me – I hate being put on the spot. I shrugged. 'Well . . . !'

'Doesn't it match Hattie's hair?' Magenta held the fuchsia fabric against Hattie's head.

'What!' Hattie growled, snatching the material away and glaring at Magenta.

'Erm . . . I'm not sure I'd say *matched* exactly,' I said.

And from the expression on Magenta's face, I got the distinct impression that that was not the answer she'd been looking for.

'How about a compromise?' Seema said.

'What sort of a compromise?' Madge asked, sounding distinctly tetchy. 'Because when my dad talks about a compromise, it usually means he gets his way and I don't get mine!'

'Blue.'

'Blue?' Magenta looked shocked.

'Yes, you know, that primary colour that goes alongside red and yellow,' Seema went on. 'Then it doesn't matter about our colouring, we could wear different shades: those with pale skin can wear dark blue and those with darker skin can wear paler blue. Problem solved!'

'Or . . .' Magenta wasn't one to give up easily. 'How about, if you lot wear blue and I wear—'

'No, Madge!' Chelsea's voice was rising and I could see why she didn't want to wear pink. Her face had already flushed puce, and it *definitely* didn't suit her! 'We've discussed this and decided we want one uniform image for the whole band. Now if you don't want to go along with that . . .'

'Fine!' Magenta said, stuffing her fabric samples into her bag. 'I'll get shades of blue then – for all of us!'

And I must say, when she showed us the drawings of her designs, I thought they looked fantastic. They're all different – Seema's outfit will be a mid blue ra-ra skirt and a tie-up silver blouse; Chelsea's is a pair of silver crop trousers and a darkish blue bodice; Hattie will be wearing a dark blue dress with a wide silver belt; Madge will be in a silver bodice and bright blue pelmet skirt and mine's the best – it's going to be a blue and silver lace tutu with a silver crop top. Ooo, I can't wait – we're all going to look fabulous. Although Mum and Dad haven't seen my costume yet, so I hope they don't think it's too revealing.

I've already had a few disappointments this term; my exam results weren't exactly brilliant for one thing, but the main one was that I really thought that, once he'd got over Magenta, Daniel Davis would ask me out again at Spud's party. But, while I was hiding under the table dodging flying doughnuts in the dining room, he was in the front room getting off with this Year 9 girl called Jodi! I was gutted when I found out. And now they seem to be an item! If only I'd gone into the sitting room to dance instead of the dining room to eat, that could've been me going out with him. Talk about being in the wrong place at the wrong time.

Anyway, last Saturday morning at the Youth Centre I was feeling pretty down about things. Our rehearsal hadn't gone very well and then Daniel was all over that Jodi girl till I couldn't bear to watch. Honestly, I don't know what's wrong with me. I mean, I know I'm not as pretty as Magenta or Seema, but it's not like I'm hideous or anything. And Ben went out with me – and he used to go out with Seema and he's now going out with Chelsea – so I can't be that bad, can I? But every time I looked over and saw them together, I was thinking, *that used to be me*. And then I'd look over in the other direction and see Daniel with his arm round Jodi Plock's shoulder and I'd be thinking, *that* could've *been me*! I was feeling pretty miserable all morning and the person I wanted there for moral support (because she hasn't got a boyfriend either since she dumped Gregory) was Madge but she'd had to go to her tutor.

Seema must've read my mind because she said, 'Just because you haven't got a boyfriend it doesn't mean there's anything wrong with you, you know, Arl.' Which was OK for her to say, because: one, she's hardly ever without a boyfriend and two, even when she is (like now) it doesn't bother her.

'I know that!' I said. 'I was just thinking about this afternoon, that's all.' Which wasn't a total lie – we'd all arranged to go round to Madge's house to have a fitting for our outfits, and I was really looking forward to it.

Daniel had to dash off early from the rehearsal because he's going to the same tutor as Madge, only he doesn't have to be there till twelve – so it was a relief when he'd gone; it meant I didn't have to watch him slobbering all over someone else.

Dead Petals were on stage when he left and Jodi Plock gave him this really casual wave. She was all, 'See ya!' trying to be all cool and detached.

'She's so pretentious,' I said to Seema.

'Who is?'

'That Emo-girl.'

'What, Jodi Plock? I think she's OK. Her dad's a psychologist who works with my mum,' Seema said.

'How come you never told me that before?'

She shook her head. 'Because Jodi Plock's parentage has never cropped up in our conversation before,' she said – which was fair enough, I suppose.

We were just gathering our things to go home when Spyro, the drummer from Spiral Thrust, came over. He's this really scruffy boy who looks as though he's been left out in the rain and his clothes have shrunk. I mean, he's bad enough in school – he looks like a pipe-cleaner in uniform – but on Saturdays when he's in his own clothes, he's even worse. His jeans are all ripped and he wears them so skinny that they're positively disgusting. He was wearing a black shirt that looked two sizes too small, so that it was bulging at the buttons, and his hair – well, don't get me started! I swear he backcombs it.

'So where's your mate today?' he asked. I looked round, thinking he must be talking to someone else. 'The one who likes wrecking classical guitar concerts?' he said in this really sarcastic way – like he was trying to jog my memory.

'Oh, Magenta.' I hoped he wasn't going to have a go at her for dumping his lead guitarist. 'She's not here.'

He gave me a look as if I'd forgotten to put my brain in this morning. 'I can see that,' he smirked. 'That's why I asked where she was.'

I felt about a centimetre tall and wanted to crawl under a chair I felt so embarrassed. 'She's at her tutor's,' I mumbled.

He raised his eyebrows. 'Her tutor's? A bit of a boffin, is she, your mate?'

Seema and I looked at each other. I didn't know quite how to answer that, so I let Seema take it. 'What's it to you?' she challenged.

'Just wondering,' he said, sounding way more defensive than when I'd spoken to him – I don't know how Seema does it. 'Anyway, here.' And he handed Seema a piece of paper with a phone number on it. 'Give this to her, will you, and tell her to ring me sometime.'

Seema took the paper and we looked at each other again.

'Are you asking her out?' Seema said, holding the paper between her thumb and forefinger as though she might catch something off it.

He gave a slight twitch of the head. 'Just tell her to ring me – OK?' Then he loped off. 'Hey, Bruno, man – OK if I leave my drum kit here till the concert? My dad says he's not carting it back and forwards every Saturday . . .'

'Give it to me,' I said to Seema. 'If Madge asks, I'll pretend I lost it.' There was no way I was going to let her get involved with that jerk.

But Seema shook her head. 'No, Arl. You know Madge, she's had the hots for him since the beginning of term. If she found out we'd interfered, she'd never let us forget it. And, look at it this way, if Daniel Davis asked Magenta to give you his number and she didn't, how would you feel?' I hadn't thought of it that way.

We started to get our things together as Bruno was winding down the rehearsal.

'OK, folks,' he shouted above the general excitement. 'If you leave any equipment here, remember that other groups do use the centre. See you next week.'

Jac Dhillon was stuffing his dhol drum into a cupboard behind the stage. 'Hey, hold on, Arlette. Will you wait for me a sec?'

'You go on, I'll catch you up,' I told Seema and the others.

When Jac came down from the stage he gave me this big grin. 'Look, I'm just wondering if . . .

well, I thought . . . maybe . . .'

Sundeep Deol gave him a shove between the shoulder blades. 'He's trying to ask you if you'll go out with him,' he laughed.

Jac looked embarrassed. 'Don't mind him; he's mad. But will you?'

I didn't know what to say. I must admit, Jac's really nice, but he's only in Year 9, so I'd never even considered him in terms of boyfriend material. He is quite funny though and definitely good looking. And, whenever anyone says anything to Magenta about her being the youngest in the year, she always says that age doesn't matter and who am I to argue?

'OK,' I agreed.

So, guess what? We're going to the pictures – tonight! There I was thinking there was something wrong with me, and look – half an hour later I've got a boyfriend again – even though he is younger than me. But, even so, I couldn't wait to tell the others.

But, by the time I caught up with them, Gregory had only gone and asked Seema out too! You see – I said she was hardly ever without a boyfriend – even ones who've turned her down once! And now she'd gone and stolen my thunder because having a boyfriend who was in Year 9 is nowhere near as exciting as having one who was not only slightly older than you but had also come back begging to be taken back after turning you down.

Anyway, we all went straight round to Magenta's house after the rehearsal for our costume fitting. I was so excited and I couldn't wait to tell her about Jac.

'But he's in Year 9!' Madge said.

'Your point?' I said – feeling more than a little bit peed off with her.

'My point is, Arl – he's younger than you!'

'And?' I said.

'Well, it's just so . . . cradle-snatchery.' She was pulling blue and silver costumes out of bin bags and laying them over the back of their settee. And, if I hadn't been feeling so annoyed with her, I'd have been speechless with how sophisticated our outfits were looking. 'First it was Daniel cradle-snatching and now you. I mean, what's going on, Arl?'

'Nothing's going on!' I snapped. The others were holding up their costumes in front of them and jumping about in excitement. 'I just like

Jac.' She seemed to have forgotten that her birthday's in August, so if she'd been born a couple of weeks later, she'd have been in Year 9 herself. And, if I'm honest, she'd touched a bit of a nerve, mentioning Daniel.

'There's no need to get so defensive,' she went on. 'I mean a boyfriend isn't everything you know. Look at me – I'm quite happy being on my own. You wouldn't get me going out with a Year 9 kid just so that I could say I was going out with someone.'

At that moment she pulled out the costume from the last bin bag. It was a froth of blue and silver lace and looked about as sophisticated as something you'd see in a little kids' dressing-up basket. I couldn't believe it! Surely that couldn't be the sexy little tutu she'd drawn for me to wear – it was hideous!

'Oh I forgot,' Seema said, holding out the scrap of paper that Spyro Evangelides had written his phone number on.

But when I saw the disgusting tutu Magenta had made for me and after all the horrible things she'd been saying about me going out with Jac, I snatched the piece of paper that Seema was holding out to her and ripped it into tiny pieces.

'If you're so happy being on your own, you won't need this then,' I yelled. I tossed the scraps of phone number at her. 'And you can keep your stupid costumes and your stupid Spangle Babes. I don't want anything to do with you or this whole stupid concert!' And I stormed out.

But the worst thing was, I thought Seema would come after me and beg me to go back and make Madge apologise for being so horrible, but she didn't. In fact, no one did. I think I might have blown my chances.

And now I don't know what to do.

9
Magenta

Oh my God! Talk about my life being like a seesaw at the moment – it's going up and down so much, I'm in danger of getting motion sickness. Take last Saturday for instance. It started off on a downer because:

1) I'd had to miss rehearsals *again*!

2) I'd had another earbashing from the Dung-beetle. Honestly – does he expect me to be psychic or something? I mean, at school, we haven't even started *The Merchant of Venice* yet, so how was I supposed to know that the main character wasn't some old-fashioned super-sleuth with a fast car? Shylock/Sherlock – it's only a couple of letters difference. And Portia/Porsche – sounds the same to me.

3) As if that wasn't bad enough, I came out to find Daniel (the mongrel) waiting outside for his lesson. And he was being sooooooo oily, he practically slithered through the door into

the kitchen. As he walked in, he was all, 'Oooo, I've done my homework, Mr Dumbarton.' And, 'Could you explain one or two points from that physics question you set me, Mr Dumbarton?' And, 'My mother took me to see *The Merchant of Venice* at the Playhouse last week and it was an excellent production.' Creep! He makes my blood boil – I don't know how I ever went out with him.

Then, in the afternoon, my seesaw went up momentarily when everyone was ooooo-ing and ah-ing at the costumes I've made for the Spangle Babes. Well, when I say *I* made, it was with a little help from Belinda – obviously. But they are my designs and anyway, what else has she got to do at the moment? It's not like she's working or anything. And let's face it, it doesn't matter how well a dress is made, without the artistic genius of the designer it'll only ever be just a dress. It's the designer (i.e. me) who makes it into a fabulous creation that everyone raves about. And that's what was happening on Saturday. So I was all – *Yay! I'm really proud and pleased that my costumes have made everyone so happy*. Until my seesaw went crashing down again!

Arlette, my so-called best friend, only went and rubbished my outfits – in front of everyone! Can you believe it? She started shouting that I was trying to make her look like the Ice Fairy and she was going to be a laughing stock! How ungrateful can you get? And all because I just happened to mention that it wasn't cool to be going out with a Year 9 boy – honestly! Some people are ridiculously oversensitive.

Of course, it wasn't long before my seesaw went up again, when Seema (who is truly my best friend now) handed me Spyro's phone number and told me that he wants me to call him! Yes! Didn't I tell you there was sparkage?

But then instantly I went crashing down into the muddy depths of despair again when Arlette snatched the number out of Seema's hand and ripped it into a gazillion teensy little pieces. I was shocked. I know Arlette can be a bit spoilt sometimes but, honestly – how mean can you get?

Anyway, it doesn't matter because Seema phoned Geeky Greg and got it from him. Apparently, Greg had gone up to her after rehearsals and asked her out. (You see, it isn't just running through our routine I miss out on, it's all the goss too! My dad is sooooo unreasonable!) Greg apologised for upsetting her and said that he really did like her but when she'd rung him up and asked him to go to Spud's party with her he'd panicked because he thought she was too good for him. Hold on a second – he asked me out, which means that he can't have thought that *I* was too good for him. Huh! The cheek of it! I must make a mental note to speak to Greg and tell him how I'm just as good as Seema in the girlfriend stakes. But, anyway, it doesn't matter because he gave Seema Spyro's number again and Spyro is way more cool than Geeky Greg.

Of course, I didn't ring Spyro straight away – I didn't want him to think I was *that* desperate. I left it at least half an hour before I phoned. And guess what? He only asked me to go to a concert with him next Saturday! And not some (boring) guitar concert at some (boring) Arts Centre either – a proper rock concert on a proper stage at the Palais with proper bouncers on the door and everything.

There is one teensy little problem though – my *un*friendly-neighbourhood Mao Tse-tung wannabe – aka Dad! The concert doesn't even start till nine o'clock so I'm going to have to come up with a pretty plausible story to keep him off the scent – otherwise he'll never let me go.

Wow! Did I say my life was a seesaw? Well it's certainly going sky high at the moment – the best thing in the world has happened. It's beyond my wildest hopes and dreams; the answer to every prayer I've ever said (in the days when I used to say my prayers – obviously); even better than winning Battle of the Bands – well, almost. My dad's going away on business! For a whole week! How amazing is that?

Gran and Auntie Venice aren't due back for another fortnight and with Dad out of the picture:

1. Belinda and I will be able to do some stress-free bonding for seven whole days. I've always wanted a mother figure in my life and Belinda's pretty cool – when Dad's not around.

And:

2. There'll be nothing standing in the way of me going to the concert – yay! I can't wait.

'Now you make sure you do everything to help Belinda.' I'd been summoned to Dad's bedroom as he packed his case. 'Don't let her lift anything and keep the house tidy so that she doesn't have to be running around after you – all right?'

'Yes, Dad.'

'And don't cause her any stress – is that clear?'

'Yes, Dad.'

'I don't really want her driving at this stage of her pregnancy, so make sure you're home at a reasonable time so that she doesn't have to go looking for you – do you understand?'

'Yes, Dad.'

'And,' as he zipped up his suitcase and lugged it downstairs, 'it might be a nice gesture if you took her breakfast in bed at the weekend, like I do – just to show your appreciation for everything she's done for you.'

Yeah, right! Like that was ever going to happen. 'Yes, Dad.'

Then the icing on the cake: 'Belinda's got a scan at the hospital on Friday and she ought to have someone with her, so I've rung the school and told them that you won't be in.' Oh yes! I gave a mental air-punch at the thought of a day off school without the pain of a sore throat or stomach cramps. I think Belinda's pregnancy is doing him good – no way would he have let me have a day off before. 'And make sure she takes a taxi.'

'Yes, Dad.'

But then he was back to his old self with one of his *I'm-warning-you* expressions. 'There's a lot of responsibility for you while I'm away, Magenta, and I'm relying on you to step up to the mark.'

I put my hand on my heart in a gesture that I hoped reflected the maturity that he was expecting from me. 'Cross my heart, cut my throat and hope to . . .'

'I'm serious, Magenta!'

'Yes, Dad. Absolutely. You can trust me.'

Belinda waddled out of the sitting room. 'Darling, the cab's here.'

'OK, off you go. Bye!' I said, leading him towards the door. 'See you next week and don't worry about a thing.'

The timing could not have been better because it meant he'd be away over the weekend and that meant I wouldn't have to invent some fictitious event that I was going to go to. Belinda's so much more laid-back than Dad: I knew she'd be OK with me going to the concert.

Although I must admit, she wasn't quite the

pushover I thought she'd be. In fact, it was more like twenty questions than the casual interest I'd hoped for, but I think I handled her well. I'd left it till the Thursday evening before I told her about Saturday night. (I have a theory that adults respond better, the less time they have to brood on things.)

'Who's performing?' She'd been sitting with her feet up on the settee.

'Erm . . . I'm not sure.' How was I supposed to know that? It's not like I'm into rock music – I was only going to this concert to be with Spyro, not because I wanted to hear the band.

'What time is he picking you up? And how are you getting there?'

She was certainly fielding me tricky ones. 'We haven't decided yet.' To be honest, I wasn't even sure if he *was* picking me up and I hadn't a clue how we were travelling.

'And what time does it end approximately?' She was rubbing her bump and staring at it in this really distracted way. 'I'll wait up for you, obviously, but Junior here needs his or her beauty sleep too, so I want you in by eleven.'

'Oh, it'll be well before eleven,' I said – pretty convincingly. I was fairly certain there was no way it would be finished by then, but I could always send her a text from the gig, couldn't I?

'OK, that's fine, but you keep your phone on at all times,' she said. Phew! I'd just settled down to watch TV, thinking that the inquisition was over, when: 'I remember Spyros Evangelides as being a bit of a disruptive element in my lessons when I taught him in Year 8. I hope he's matured with age.'

I looked her straight in the eye. 'You wouldn't recognise him.' I had my fingers crossed behind my back, although, strictly speaking, I hadn't actually told a lie. After all, he's got long hair now and a little goatee (not like Mr Marlowe's disgusting dead-slug type thing; Spyro's is really cute and sexy) and he must be nearly six feet tall – so it was true – no way would Belinda recognise him from the little kid she'd taught in Year 8.

'Good,' she said, rubbing her tummy again. 'Now, you wouldn't be a darling and make me a cup of peppermint tea, would you? I've got terrible heartburn.'

See – piece of cake! In fact, if I play my cards right, I might even be able to talk her into letting me off the Dung-beetle's on Saturday morning. And of course the next day was the day of her hospital appointment and my day off school. Oh yes – I think Dad should go away more often.

I must say, I thought our stress-free bonding session was going brilliantly. In fact, I was starting to think of Belinda more like an older sister than a stepmother and I'm pretty sure the feeling was mutual because, as we were following blue arrows painted on to the pukey green walls of the hospital corridor, she started to confide in me about some gigs she'd been to when she was my age – well, ish.

'This was really naughty . . .' she giggled as we went into the hospital shop. 'But some friends and I actually scaled the perimeter fence at Glastonbury.' Then she looked very shamefaced. 'Of course, it was completely unethical and I would never do it again, but at the time we just wanted to get in and security was nowhere near as tight as it is now. Do you want anything?' she asked, picking up a tube of mints.

I handed her a magazine. 'You went to Glastonbury? Ugh!' No way would I be seen within a welly's throw of that mud-fest. School summer camp was bad enough without pitching a tent in a swamp for fun!

Belinda laughed again. 'It's not muddy every

year.' Yeah, right! That's not what it looks like from the coverage on my TV. 'We had some great experiences. You should try it one y—' Then she grabbed my shoulder, leant forward and started to pant like Sirius, my dog, does when he wants a treat.

'Ohmigod! You're not having it now, are you?'

'That'll be two pounds thirty, please,' the man behind the counter said – like women gave birth in his shop every day.

'Can't you see she's having a baby?' I growled at him. 'Call an ambulance! Call a doctor! Call anyone!'

Belinda straightened up and smiled. 'It's fine. These aren't labour pains yet – there's another three weeks to go.'

I threw some money on the counter, grabbed the mints and my mag and pulled Belinda towards the main hospital.

'Come on, let's get you to where there are people who know what they're doing if this thing decides to come early.' I glared at the man with my best *you-are-a-total-waste-of-space* look.

Of course, on the positive side, at least if she did have the baby now, she would be in a hospital, which is what Dad's wanted all along. Belinda, on the other hand, has been hell-bent on having a water-birth at home from the start. I've heard her and Dad arguing about it. She says she wants it to be born in a natural environment. Hmmm! I'm thinking – a paddling pool in the sitting room? Yeah, right, because that is soooooo natural. And anyway, *Maison Orange*, a natural environment? I don't think so! It would stand a better chance of a normal upbringing if it was born into the Hammer House of Horrors.

Belinda was walking along the corridor. 'Trust me, the baby is not coming just yet – and, by the way, he or she is a human, not a *thing*.' Baby/thing – whatever! 'These pains are called Braxton Hicks contractions and they're just my body practising.'

'Well it freaks me out when you do that,' I pointed out. Honestly – the more I see what Belinda's going through, the more I have definitely decided on adoption when I have kids.

She smiled at me and rubbed my hand. 'Thank you for coming with me today. I don't want you to be worried. Really, it's no different from you practising your dance routine for the contest,' she said.

Which gave me a very timely lead into my next request. 'Speaking of which . . .' I began, as I hooked my arm through hers in a supportive gesture. After all, she was upright again and waddling at a steady pace, so I thought I should go for it while she was in full gratitude mode. 'I haven't actually had much chance to practise with the others because of going to Mr Dumbarton's every week and it's the final run-through on Saturday. I don't want to let the rest of them down, so I was wondering . . .'

'Nice try, Magenta, but no. Your dad left very clear instructions that you shouldn't miss your tutor,' she said as we reached the waiting room.

There were only three seats left in the waiting room, one over by the water machine, which Belinda took, and two others on the opposite side of the room. And believe me, I was happy to put some distance between us. She pretends to be all cool and understanding but underneath she's caught the Dad-bug just like the rest of the adults in my world. One of the chairs had a sign taped to the seat saying BROKEN. DO NOT USE, so I sat on the one next to it and buried my head in my magazine. Hmph! So much for our stress-free bonding!

We were in there for ages: it was sooooo boring. And hot! Honestly, it was like a sauna in there. After about half an hour, I put my magazine down on the chair next to me and went over to get a cup of water from the machine.

I had my back to the room and didn't notice that a hugely pregnant woman had come in with her husband. As I turned round to go back to my seat I saw that he'd only gone and sat on it! Cheek! But then – uh-oh! I realised that his wife had sat down next to him – on the chair that was out of use. Only she probably hadn't been able to see the sign saying it was broken because I'd put my magazine down on it – ooops!

I was just about to tell her, when a nurse popped her head round the door and said, 'Belinda Lovell?'

Lovell? I was shocked. Surely Belinda was an Orange since she'd married Dad – not literally, of course, but you know what I mean. Why was this nurse still calling her by her maiden name?

Before I could ask her, there was a wailing sound from the other side of the waiting room. I looked over and saw the legs of the broken chair splaying outwards and the pregnant woman sitting on it slithering very slowly towards the ground.

I grabbed Belinda's arm and heaved her to her feet.

'Come on,' I said, dragging her towards the door. But then all hell let loose:

1) There was a loud crack as one of the legs snapped right off the chair and the woman toppled over and started flapping about like a turtle that had gone belly up.

2) She gave another howl and it looked like she'd peed her pants because there was liquid everywhere (gross!). Her husband started shouting about breaking water or something – but I was thinking, *Durr! Water's a liquid – you can't break a liquid.* Even *I* know that and I'm rubbish at science! (But I thought I'd better move away from the water dispenser, just in case.)

3) Then the woman started groaning and panting, like Belinda had been doing in the corridor, only a zillion times worse. (Seriously – there is no dignity in having babies. Now I know God must be a man – because a woman would have made childbirth way more cool.)

4) Nurses and orderlies started dashing about,

trying to heave this poor woman on to a trolley. Honestly – what a palaver. It was worse than when I dropped a lump of margarine on the floor in Food Technology in Year 8 and Mrs Blobby trod on it. She careered the length of the room on one leg like a ballerina in a fat suit, before she got wedged between Arlette's and Billy O'Dowd's work stations. It took Fred, the school-keeper, and two of his assistants ten minutes to prise her free.

'Magenta?' Belinda was giving me that weird look. I had an uneasy feeling that the next question would be something along the lines of *have you got anything to do with this?*

I ushered her out into the corridor and opened my arms in a gesture of innocence.

'I was nowhere near her,' I protested. After all, was it my fault if the staff were too lazy to remove a faulty chair? I don't think so!

The nurse who'd called Belinda opened the door to a side room.

'Just wait in there till the radiographer comes,' she said to us, then disappeared back into the waiting room to help the pregnant woman.

The room was really tiny and the blinds were drawn, making it seem dark and dingy. There were a couple of computer type things: one on the side and another on wheels in front of a weird-looking bed. To be honest, it looked more like some medieval torture chamber than a room that babies are born in.

'I'm not surprised you want to have the baby at home, if this is the sort of place they expect you to have it. Talk about depressing!' I said, picking up a plastic bottle that was on a tray next to the bed.

'This isn't where the babies are born; this is just where they do the scans. Leave that alone please, Magenta,' Belinda said, climbing up on to the couch.

'What is it? Glue?' I took the lid off and pressed the sides of the bottle to make a blob come out of the nozzle.

She chuckled. 'No, it's lubricating jelly to help the scanner move over my abdomen.'

But just then a light flickered on and a voice boomed from the doorway, 'DON'T touch anything!'

'Aaaaggggh!' I yelled, startled.

But as I jumped, I accidentally squeezed the plastic tube. A flume of transparent lubricating jelly shot about a metre into the air then came down, splat on the floor, just at the spot the radiographer plonked her foot down. One leg skidded forwards while her arms windmilled backwards and cracked against the computer that was on the trolley, sending it whizzing into the other computer that was on the side bench. The woman reached out and grabbed a sheaf of cables to steady herself. But unfortunately they were attached to the static computer. The whole thing teetered on the edge of the bench for a second then smashed down on to the wheelie one before both computers hit the floor in a (quite impressive, actually) mini pyrotechnic display.

Honestly! Belinda has so made the right decision about a home birth. I don't know what my dad was thinking of, wanting my little brother or sister to be born in this place. What with collapsing chairs and exploding computers, it's like a war zone in there!

Actually, when they eventually found someone else to do Belinda's scan in a different room, the radiographer said she could tell whether it was a boy or girl. But Belinda said she didn't want to know until Dad got back. I was a teensy bit disappointed at first, but I suppose it's only fair really.

You should have seen it on the screen though – I mean, there was more than a passing resemblance to ET but it was quite cute. It had teensy little fingers and it was sucking its thumb and scratching its nose and everything – just like a real baby.

Only three weeks to go till I'm a big sister. Ooooooo! I can't wait.

10
Daniel

Man-o-man! Have I got a problem: I've got girls coming out of my ears! (Not literally, you understand.) I know most boys would think that this was like being in heaven, but it's beginning to be a bit of a pain.

1. Arlette has been homing in on me like some sort of human heat-seeking missile every break time and phoning me up most evenings to tell me what a cow Magenta is being – apparently they've had some sort of row about the Battle of the Bands and they're not speaking. (But I guarantee, they'll be best buds again by next week – girls are like that.) I'm sure it's all a ploy to try and get off with me and yet she's supposed to be going out with this kid in Year 9 – so what's that about?

2. Jodi Plock *isn't* all over me! In fact, she's being really cool and laid-back about us and this weird relationship we're supposed to be having – which is confusing me even more

than Arlette's constant in-your-face stuff. I mean, I know Jodi likes me because all her mates have told me – in emails, texts, notes – it's even written in the boys' bogs! And yet, she's being so *if-you-phone-me-you-phone-me: if-you-don't-you-don't* that I haven't a clue whether or not she gives a monkey's about us.

3. Magenta's cousin Justine has been emailing me – again! Things went quiet on that front after we'd been on holiday last year, but I think the Orange family grapevine must have got wind that Magenta and I are over, because ever since Christmas, Justine's been sending me funny messages on Netlog.

And, scariest of all:

4. Margaret (Dad's girlfriend's eldest daughter), who had her thirteenth birthday party while I was over there last time, was all, 'Let's play spin the bottle; Daniel, you sit opposite me.' And, 'Let's play true, dare, kiss or promise. Daniel, I dare you to kiss me.' Which isn't how it's supposed to work anyway!

'Just sit back and enjoy it, blud,' Magnus said when we were putting the finishing touches to our track on the Friday night before the final run-through for Battle of the Bands. 'Most blokes would kill to be in your position.'

'Not when you don't fancy the girls,' I replied.

'What about the weird and wonderful Lodi Miss Jodi? You must fancy her.' Magnus was wiring the sound module into the back of my computer.

Spud had also come round – more to be next door to Magenta than to help with the music, I suspected. 'Yeah – Jodi Plock rocks! Hey, hey! I am a poet and I didn't know it.' He pulled out a digital camera from his pocket. 'Hey, Danno, when you've finished your music, can I download some photos on to your computer? Dad won't let me near his since I accidentally destroyed some of his client files from work, and I wanted to print out some of Magenta from the holiday last year.'

'No probs,' I said, setting the sound module to the computer so that everything we'd put into the track would be synchronised.

'Seriously,' Magnus went on. 'What about you and Jodi?'

I shrugged. 'I'm telling you – I don't know where I am with her. One minute she's getting all deep and meaningful, the next she walks past me like I'm someone she once saw at a bus stop, and then she presents me with tickets to see Jagged Edge in concert tomorrow night at the Palais.'

'You going?'

'Probably.' After all, Jodi and I hadn't really been out properly since the party – only in school and at the Youth Centre on Saturdays, when we were practising anyway – so it would be a chance to see if I really did like her or if, as Mum said, I was just on the rebound from Magenta. And as Jodi's dad had bought the tickets for her, it wasn't like I was going to have to pay or anything, so what had I got to lose? I sat down in front of the computer. 'OK – are we ready?'

I let our track play and we all sat back and listened. It was sounding really good, although I could hear that it wasn't quite there yet.

'That drum loop still isn't right,' Magnus commented.

'I could download a plug-in from the Net and add it over the top,' I suggested. 'How about some tribal drums?'

We played around with different drum plug-ins till it was turned ten o'clock and we were exhausted.

'Look, let's just do it as far as we've got tomorrow, then we've got another week before the actual competition,' I said, saving the file and unplugging the sampler and sound module.

'Can I use the computer now?' Spud asked, almost knocking me out of the way to plug his camera into the USB point.

'Don't mind me,' I said. 'Magnus and I need to go through the visuals for tomorrow anyway.'

While Magnus and I were discussing the slide show that was going to accompany the soundtrack, Spud began downloading his photographs and printing some of them out. I looked across and, I must admit, it was really weird seeing pictures of Magenta in her bikini when it was freezing outside. And I couldn't help thinking how happy she looked. There she was on the screen, lying on the beach smiling that big smile of hers, which really was gorgeous. And her eyes were sparking. She could look very beautiful.

I felt the beginnings of a lump in my throat – which was probably due to tiredness; it was getting very late. I swallowed hard and turned my attention to Magnus again. But out of the corner of my eye, I could see another photo, this time it was of the two of us together: I was standing behind Magenta with my arms round her waist and she had leaned her head back against my chest. We both looked so happy. And, actually, we *were* happy. I sighed. Magnus was talking about images and colours and gels but I was lying there wondering what had happened to make it all go so pear-shaped between the two of us.

'Neh! Don't want that one,' Spud muttered, deleting the one of Magenta and me before I could say anything – not that I wanted to keep it, you understand, but it seemed a shame to get rid of it all together.

The next one was Magenta on the beach in that little pink top she wore. It really suited her. And then there were some more of her sunbathing.

'Didn't you take pictures of anything else on your holiday?' Magnus asked.

Spud thought for a moment. 'Not really.'

Magnus shook his head. 'You are seriously obsessed – you know that?'

'Nothing wrong with a bit of healthy obsession,' Spud said, printing out the one of Magenta in her shades. 'I'm aiming to have my whole bedroom wallpapered with these.'

Just then there was a knock on my French windows.

'Quick,' I whispered to Spud. 'Get rid of them. That's Magenta and if she sees these she'll do her pieces.'

Magnus and I began frantically gathering up the printouts.

'Can I save them on to your computer?' Spud said.

'OK, but just be quick about it.' I stuffed the photos under my futon mattress and waited for Spud to unplug his camera from the USB point. Then I nonchalantly pulled up the blind to see Magenta, shivering on the balcony with her bathrobe pulled round her. I opened the French window and she stepped into the warmth.

'Daniel,' she said, 'I am trying to get an early night and you lot are keeping me awake.'

'Hi, Magenta!' Spud called from the other side of the room.

'Can you please keep the noise down; I have a very important day tomorrow,' she went on.

'That's fine – the lads are going in a minute. It's a pretty big day for all of us with the final run-through and everything,' I said.

'Hi, Magenta!' Spud said again, even louder.

'I wasn't talking about the run-through. I'm

going to a concert tomorrow night – a proper one, at the Palais – with Spyro,' she said.

'Me too – not with Spyro, obviously, but with . . .' I began, but then I noticed the line of Magenta's sight had gone down to where my bed meets the floor. I followed it and saw a piece of paper sticking out. And on the paper I could just make out a foot, with painted toenails and an ankle bracelet – a very distinctive ankle bracelet because it had little red hearts all round and it was the one I'd bought her last summer. Uh-oh!

'What's that?' she said, snatching the photograph out from under the futon mattress. It was the one of her in that pretty deep pink bikini with twinkly bits all over it that made her look so fabulous on holiday.

'It's not what you think,' I said, looking to Spud for some support.

'I'll tell you what I think!' she boomed, ripping up the photo and throwing the pieces in my face. 'I think you're a pathetic pervert!' Then she stormed back towards her own bedroom. 'And there'd better not be any more like that – anywhere!' she yelled along the balcony.

Magnus slapped me on the shoulder and

grinned. 'You might be pathetic, my old china, but no way are you a pervert.' He looked towards Spud who was gazing at the French window with a smile like a man who'd had his brain removed. 'Now, if you want to talk perverts . . .'

'Wow!' Spud sighed. 'That is one seriously fiery babe. I am so hot for her right now!'

I am so mad, I can't even speak! Magnus and I had called our music track – you know, that track that it's taken us three weeks to create, every evening, weekend and every moment we could get together – i.e. every waking moment of our lives for the past twenty-one days . . . Sorry, I'm so angry, I've digressed. Anyway, we'd called it Sunbathing. As in bathing in Sun – as in Acid House/Sun. Get it? And it was filed on my computer under that name. (Do you see where I'm going with this?)

So, when it was Luminance's turn to go up on stage for the last run-through before the sound check next week, what happened when I tried to find the track? IT'D GONE! Totally erased. Nothing but a load of squiggles on my screen.

'WHAT!' I screamed.

'Where is it?' Magnus yelled.

We were standing on the stage in a state of shock. Then we both turned and looked at Spud and said, through gritted teeth, 'What did you do with our music last night?'

He looked up and pulled his dumb-ass face. 'I didn't do anything to your music. I was just printing out pictures of Magenta.'

'And you saved them under what name?' I snarled.

'Sunbathing,' he said. ' 'Cos that's what she was doing. Is it a problem?'

'Is it . . . ! What the . . . I mean . . . how in . . .' I was speechless with rage.

Magnus took over. 'Spud – our track was a Cubase file and your photos were jpgs. How the hell did you manage to completely wipe out one with the other?'

He shrugged. 'I guess I'm just technically gifted that way.'

Gggggrrrrr!

So, yet again, my life is completely pants:

1. Thanks to Sam No-brain Pudmore, Magnus and I have got exactly one week to re-create our track before the competition next

Saturday. And – before you ask – no, it wasn't backed up anywhere!

2. I'm supposed to be going to the gig tonight with Jodi, but I don't think I'm going to have time. Magnus has said that he'll carry on working on the track while I'm out, but it hardly seems fair to leave him grafting while I'm off raving, does it?

And,

3. I never want to set eyes on Spud ever again – or Magenta! Because if she hadn't come round moaning about the noise we were making, Spud would never have panicked and saved the photos in a hurry and destroyed our music.

I can't believe I even started to think about Magenta in *that* way again last night. I can only think I must have been delusional through work-exhaustion. Maybe I should go out with Jodi after all – take my mind off everything else.

Yep! I deserve a bit of a break – mosh pit, here I come!

11

Magenta

Wow – how adult am I? Spyro's brother is only going to drive us to the concert in his car! Without any parents in there or anything! Ooooo – I can't wait.

But, actually I'm getting ahead of myself because guess what? This morning Belinda let me go to the first hour of the dress rehearsals at the Youth Centre and then dash off to the Dung-beetle's for a single one-hour session. She said it was a compromise. Didn't I tell you she was a pushover?

And the rehearsal went amazingly well – considering that Arlette was still being a complete pain in the bum. She totally spat her dummy out as we were getting changed in the girls' toilets.

'I am not wearing it!' she said, tossing down the tutu that I'd designed for her. 'If you think it looks so good, *you* wear it.' She grabbed the bag containing the stylish blue pelmet skirt and silver bodice I was going to wear. 'And I'll wear yours.'

I snatched it back from her. 'All the costumes

were made to fit the individuals.'

'So what are you saying?' She pulled the bag towards her again.

'I'm saying . . .' I yanked it back again, '. . . that your skirt was made to your measurements and this was made to mine.'

'You're supposed to be the costume designer,' she snapped. 'Alter it!' She heaved at the bin bag again and it split, spilling my lovely pelmet and bodice on to the disgustingly gross floor of the toilets.

'You stupid idiot!' I yelled at her, picking up my outfit and dusting it down.

'*You're* a stupid idiot and you design stupid clothes.' Honestly, Arlette is soooooo childish. 'And anyway, our different measurements have never been an issue whenever you've wanted to borrow something of mine before. I wonder why that is?' She scratched her chin and pulled this pretend thinking face. 'Oh yes – BECAUSE WE'RE THE SAME SIZE!' She reached out and grabbed the hem of my skirt. Seriously – I don't know what's got into her. I've never seen Arl so hostile – it must be this Year 9 boy she's 'going out' with – immaturity by association.

'Give it back!' I caught the waistline and tried to wrench it out of Arl's hands but she was holding on to it as though it was made of gold.

We were both grappling with my pelmet in this tug-of-war kind of way, until Seema stepped in between us. 'Oh for heaven's sake – the pair of you!' Whoa! Who did she think she was, my dad? 'Give it to me while there's a costume left to fight over.' We both stopped and handed the skirt to Seema. 'Now,' she said, looking from one to the other. 'Magenta, your design wasn't stupid; it was fantastic . . .'

'Thank you!' I said, putting my hands on my hips and giving Arlette a look that told her she was totally out of order.

'But . . .' Seema went on, '. . . if Arl doesn't feel comfortable in it, there's no point in making her wear it.' Then Arl did this really pathetic thing of folding her arms and smirking in a superior way, like she'd won a point or something – as if! 'So, as lead singer of Spangle Babes, I'm going to pull rank and tell you to swap skirts . . .'

'But . . .' I protested.

'Wait!' Seema held up her hand like she'd suddenly morphed into some sort of fascist traffic controller. 'Madge, if you don't feel comfortable in it either then, as our backing dancer, you can wear something different from the rest of us.' She looked across to the wash basins where the others were sitting. 'What does everyone think?'

There was an enthusiastic, 'Yes,' from Arl (of course!) and some muttered 'Suppose so,'s from Chelsea and Hattie.

'Does that mean I can wear pink?' I asked. (Dad might have a lot of faults, but he's always impressed upon me the need to make quite sure of the small print before I agree to anything.)

Chelsea groaned and Hattie rolled her eyes.

'If it really doesn't feel right, then OK – as a last resort – you could wear pink,' Seema said. 'Now, we've got to work together and I think we'd all feel a lot more like a team if the two of you kissed and made up.'

Arlette and I both said sorry and, actually, Arlette had been right. I put on the tutu and it really didn't do anything for me. Which meant that now I can wear my pink ra-ra skirt after all. Honestly, if the others had just listened to me in the first place and let me wear a contrasting outfit, all this could've been avoided. It's a good job I'm into this whole *being the bigger person* thing; anyone else would've done an *I-told-you-so*, but I was very adult about it all. And I can't help feeling that it is so the right thing for the band. We are going to look absolutely fantastic next week.

I was a bit sad that I didn't have a proper costume for the dress rehearsal, but it still went OK. I only mimed the wrong words once or twice and I don't think I made a single mistake on the dancing. In fact, I felt extremely pleased with the choreography.

I must admit, it was nice to be there for once and see what everyone else was doing. Of course, Spyro was looking as totally fabulous as ever. He was being soooooo laid-back. He just breezed past me and said casually, 'You still up for tonight?' Like it was no big deal. He is so cool.

Daniel's lot were total losers – as always. They didn't even have a track to play, so we all had to sit there watching these pictures of bombs and babies and weird bubbly blobs flashing all round the hall for five minutes because the sound had gone. Typical!

And as for that little Bride of Dracula girlfriend of his! She was wearing a bodice that is almost exactly the same design as mine, only mine is silver and sophisticated, while hers is cream with little black rosebuds stitched into it and a black edging. I mean, how morbid is that? And she had a black lace tutu with little ballet pumps. Talk about Freaks Anonymous!

I was quite relieved I had to leave early to go to the Dung-beetle's so I missed her actual performance. Of course, it also meant that I missed Spiral Thrust's performance too – but I bet they were brilliant. I've decided, if Spangle Babes don't win next week, Spiral Thrust are my second favourites. Or, better still, we could tie for first place. And then we could do gigs together and maybe a talent scout from one of the big record labels will see us and sign us up and we'll go touring the country together on one of those big buses that bands have and Spyro and I will be in all the tabloids like Posh and Becks or Katie and Peter. How rock and roll would that be? And our first step on the road to stardom is tonight's concert! I am sooooooo excited.

Spyro? Huh! Psycho, more like! That boy is a complete nutcase and I don't want anything to do with him ever again. Belinda was right – he *is* a disruptive influence (not that I would ever let her know that!). He has totally ruined my evening – and my costume for the Battle of the Bands – in fact, he's ruined my entire life!

To start with, when I rang up and asked him what I should wear, he let out this really horrible tut and said, 'Durr! Clothes.' I mean, how unhelpful is that? Anyway, as Daniel had told me he was going with his little emu, or whatever she calls herself, I went round to ask him. And he was hardly any better. He just shrugged and said, 'Jeans and a T-shirt.' What is it with everyone that when I ask for advice on the dress code for an event, they come up with 'jeans and whatever'? Seema did it at the Arts Centre, and now Daniel. Honestly! Doesn't anyone care about making a good impression any more?

In the end, I decided to wear my silver bodice (the one I designed for Spangle Babes) with the pink ra-ra skirt that I was probably going to wear for the contest (because it will look so much better than the blue tutu). The reason my pink ra-ra is my fave skirt in the whole world is – apart from the sequins that are sewn round the bottom of the frill that make it twinkle in the light – that it's really unusual; instead of having a couple of frills stitched in layers like most ra-ras, it has one long frill that starts at the waist and spirals (Gggrrrr! I hate using that word – it reminds me of the demon drummer from Hell!) downwards over my hips to the hem. It has that sort of Latin look to it – and I love it – or at least I did!

I got an inkling that things weren't quite right when Spyro called to pick me up. In fact, I could hardly believe he was being so horrible to me. He didn't say how nice I looked or anything; he just grunted and flicked his head in the direction of the clapped-out rust bucket that was revving up in the middle of the road.

Belinda gave me an anxious frown. 'You're sure you've got your phone?'

'Yep!' I tapped the side of my bag and tried to usher her back indoors. 'Bye!' It was social suicide to have an ex-teacher in your house, let alone waving you off at the door.

'Well, don't be afraid to ring me if you're at all worried – about anything.'

'Absolutely. Bye,' I said, trying both to reassure her and get her out of sight of Spyro.

But then she stepped out of the door and called down the path, 'Spyros!'

He turned round, like a little boy who'd been caught out. 'Yes, Ms Lovell?'

'You take good care of Magenta – do you understand?'

'Will do, Ms Lovell!'

Oh dear God! How embarrassing was that? No wonder Spyro couldn't wait to get to the car. But then, instead of sitting next to me, he jumped in the front and left me to get in the back – without even opening the door for me. Can you believe it? I mean, it's not that I'm incapable of opening the door myself, but on a first date it would be quite nice to see that the boy actually appreciates and respects me.

As I got in there was a disgusting musty smell and I could hear weird throaty noises like a suction pump unblocking a drain. 'Have you got a dog in here, or something?' I asked, peering inside.

Spyro didn't answer. Instead he turned round and handed me a ticket. 'Let me introduce you – this is my big bro, Stavros.' He nodded towards the driver. Then he handed another ticket to this shadow of a figure who was sitting huddled in the corner at the back. 'And this is my little bro, Petros.' I almost leapt out of my skin when I realised there was another person in there next to me. 'You probably know him better as Pete. I'm sure you've seen him around school.'

I screwed up my eyes to try and see if I recognised him but his hoody was pulled right over his eyes. I must admit, I hadn't even realised that Spyro had any brothers, never mind one who was at our school.

'Hi, Pete,' I said, into the dark. 'I don't think we know each other. Whose tutor group are you in?'

There was this disgustingly snotty snort. 'Miss Crumm's.'

Eeeewww! Now I knew who he was – Miss Crumm is our rhinoceros of a PE teacher and also a form tutor in Year 9, which meant that my backseat travelling companion was none other than the nasally challenged nerd, (un)affectionately known as Peter Peter the bogey eater. I don't wish to be too graphic at this point, but it's because of the disgusting way he picks his nose and . . . well, I'm sure you can imagine the rest.

I shuffled as far as I could to the other end of

the seat and stared out of the window till we got to the Palais.

'Cheers, bro!' Spyro leapt out of the car and gave a wave to Stavros as he walked towards the entrance.

Stavros turned round to the back seat. 'Now, you two – I want you back here at eleven thirty on the dot. I'm not hanging around, understand?'

Stavros said something in Greek and Pete rumbled another throaty gurgle, as though he was trying to dislodge half a tonne of phlegm, then gave his brother the thumbs-up.

I wasn't sure why Spyro had walked off and left me with Mucus-boy, so I ran across the forecourt till I caught up with him.

'Hold on. Wait for me!' I yelled, grabbing the sleeve of his shirt. 'Have I done something to upset you?' I knew it was a long shot, but I couldn't think of any other reason for him to walk off like that.

He raised his hands to shoulder height and stepped back. 'Hey, easy! This is my best moshing T-shirt – I don't want it ripped before I've even been body-surfing.'

'I just wanted to know why you walked off and

left me.' We edged our way towards the front of the queue.

'Look, Magnet-er – or whatever your name is – my job is done. OK? My little bro wanted to go out with you, so I set it up. You got a problem with that?'

What! I could hardly believe my ears.

'Er – yes, I have a problem with it: one, your little brother is gross! And two, you asked me to come to the concert with *you*!'

Spyro raised his eyebrows. 'Yeah, right! Like I'd be seen dead with some little pretty-in-pink Barbie-doll like you.' Cheek! I was never into Barbie – I was much more a Bratz girl when I was young. But it was nice that he at least recognised the fact that I did look pretty when I wore pink. It was probably the nearest I'd got to a compliment from him. 'I asked you if you wanted to see Jagged Edge,' he went on. 'I didn't ask if you wanted to see them with *me*.' And he walked off into the crowd – just like that!

I didn't know what to do. It was only just turned nine o'clock, so I could hardly phone Belinda and ask her to come and pick me up. She wouldn't actually say *I told you Spyros Evangelides was a bad influence* – she would just look at me with one of those pitying expressions that says *who's been a silly girl, then?*

Maybe, I thought, I could get a lift to Seema's or Arlette's. I turned round to try and ask Stavros before he could drive off, but ohmigod – Phlegm-Face was heading straight towards me and just behind him were Daniel and the emu. I did another one-eighty-degree pivot before any of them could see me and headed back to the concert. After all, I had a ticket; I might as well use it.

I merged with the rest of the people piling into the Palais – and, honestly, they might as well have been going to a funeral – in Cardboard City! They were all in black – with the occasional hint of purple or red from the girls – and scruffy wasn't the word! At the door, boys were being pushed to one side and girls to the other. I followed the other girls to where a woman the size of a bus shelter started frisking me.

'Whoa!' I yelled. 'What are you doing?' I'm sure that constitutes common assault.

'Bag!' snapped the woman.

'Cow!' I said back – no one was going to insult me in public.

'Open – your – bag,' she snarled.

Ooops! I opened my bag and she scrabbled through it like she was at a jumble sale. Honestly, don't these people have any respect for other people's property?

But if I thought that was bad, once I was through the doors it was like emerging into hell. The music was already blaring out – and believe me, it was sooooooo not my type of music. It was pitch dark in there, with bodies heaving and leaping about everywhere. Suddenly, I was caught up in a swirling mass that was like being squeezed through a funnel. I was being bashed from all sides with elbows in my face and ribs and feet stamping on mine. It was worse than when Up Front has a sale on.

'Ouch! Get off me!' I screamed, but no one could hear because the music was so loud.

Then someone grabbed my legs and before I knew what was happening I was lifted up in the air.

'Aaaaggghh! Put me down!'

But everyone ignored me. People were pushing me over their heads towards the stage, like in that kiddies' game where you bat the balloon to each other. I was completely helpless. And then I felt my bag falling off my shoulder into the crowd.

'Stop! Stop!' I screamed. But they didn't. I tried to put my foot down, but all that managed to achieve was the loss of my shoes. I was being propelled over the heads of the pulsating crowd, rolling round and round like a lump of meat on a rotisserie. Help! I felt seasick. And then I became aware of a slackening sensation round my hips – uh-oh! I definitely did not like the feel of that.

Other things were being tossed around the room as well as me – water bottles, shoes, belts and – wait a minute – I was sure I recognised that! A ribbon of sparkly pink fabric sailed across my field of vision as I continued on my journey across the heads of the crowd. Oh no! I was pretty sure that it wasn't just coincidence that it had more than a passing resemblance to the frill of my ra-ra skirt. I tried to reach down and feel my skirt, but all that was left was a strip of fabric about the width of my hand – the whole of the beautiful spiral frill had disappeared.

Just as suddenly as I'd been lifted up and over the heads of the crowd, I was dropped down again into the middle of this heaving mass of hardcore moshers, all bouncing and jumping about and kicking me and trampling on me. Something wet was dropping on my head and I hoped it was nothing more disgusting than water from the dozens of bottles flying about. I couldn't believe people actually came here for pleasure.

I knew I had to get out before I was trampled to death, so I scrabbled through the forest of legs to the front where the stage was and levered myself on to my feet. Phew! Uh-oh – too soon! An enormous bouncer saw me and started gesticulating towards the crowd.

'Get back,' he mouthed.

He had *got* to be kidding me: no way was I risking life and limb in there again! I did a recce for an escape route, but the only exits meant negotiating the mayhem of the mosh pit. Then I saw my chance. There was one of those signs with the little green running man at the side of the stage. Of course! There had to be an exit backstage otherwise it would be a fire hazard. That was it – that would be my way out. I'd already lost half my clothes as well as my accessories; I needed to get out of there before I lost my life as well.

But just as I got my first knee up on to the stage to clamber to freedom, the bouncer caught the hem of what was left of my skirt and tried to pull me back down. I put my foot on his chest and tried to push him away – I was determined to escape; after all, I didn't care if I got thrown out; in fact, if I did that would solve my problem very nicely, thank you!

But as I pushed the bouncer away and levered myself on to the stage, there was a finale of drum roll, a crash of cymbals and the song came to an end. In the split second before the applause started, all that could be heard was the sound of ripping fabric.

I stood up and looked down at the bouncer. He was standing there with a face like a rabid Rottweiler and in his hand a rag of pink fabric – all that was left of my best ra-ra skirt – ooops!

Suddenly, the spotlight focused on me and I realised I was standing on the stage in nothing but my silver bodice and my really huge PE knickers. (All my thongs were in the wash today, thank goodness – Belinda always says that there's a bright side to everything.)

A roar went up from the crowd and then they started chanting: 'Jump, jump, jump!'

Yeah, right! I might have been totally humiliated,

but I didn't have a death-wish. But, when I looked round, the bouncer was starting to climb up on stage after me, and believe me, I've seen happier-looking lions stalking their prey. Uh-oh! There was nothing else for it – I closed my eyes, took a deep breath and dived out into the crowd. I adopted the star position, because I thought, the bigger I can make myself, the more likely it is that people will catch me. And they did! Phew! A sea of hands propelled me over their heads again, only this time I was going towards the back of the room and, hopefully, safety.

I spent the rest of the evening in the ladies, until it got to near the end, then I thought I might see someone I knew leaving and get a lift home, so I wandered outside into the freezing cold. There I was, sitting on the pavement outside the Palais in my underwear and shivering for Britain. What a night! I'd lost my:

1. date
2. skirt
3. shoes
4. bag – which, by the way, also meant I'd lost my

5. phone and
6. money!

But probably the most devastating loss of the night was:

7. my dignity!

And, to rub salt into my (multiple) wounds, just at that moment, I heard a familiar voice behind me.

'Magenta? You OK? Where's Spyro?'

Oh great! It was Daniel and the emu come to gloat. My cup of happiness was full!

12
Daniel

Wow! The concert was amazing! Talk about being on a high! Everyone was leaping about in the mosh pit and head-banging; bottles of water were flying everywhere; people were crowd surfing and stage diving – I've never experienced anything like it. It totally blew me away!

Even Magenta got into the spirit of the gig. You should've seen her, riding across the crowd like a surfing pro! And, when the supporting band finished, I looked up and there she was, standing in the spotlight, preparing to stage dive. And you should've seen what she was wearing – she looked fantastic in this really cool bodice and hot pants. I'd never have seen Magenta as someone who'd be into that sort of thing. I was well impressed – and, weirdly enough, also a bit sad.

I mean, five weeks ago, I'd have bet anything on the fact that I knew Magenta inside out: her taste in music, clothes – even other boys. But since we split, we just seem to have drifted so far apart. It's like she's a stranger to me, which is the really sad part considering how close we've been for over ten years. Although, on the positive side, she looked out of this world and really let her hair down so that I saw a totally different side to her – a side that I liked, may I add!

Don't get me wrong, Jodi was great company, but I was a tad disappointed that she didn't join in much. She just stood on the side with a bottle of water, nodding her head in time to the music. Which was cool – but it would've been nice if she'd let herself go a bit.

We had to leave before the end because Jodi's dad was coming to pick us up at eleven thirty. Her dad's an educational psychologist who pretends to be one of these 'right on' parents. He likes to think he's in touch with his kids, but the reality is, he's a dad, just like any other parent, which he proved when he wouldn't let her stay an extra half hour. If he was really in touch with 'the youth of today' he'd have known that the climax of every set is the last song, and we had to miss it. I didn't go on about it though, because I think Jodi was a bit embarrassed – not that she'd ever admit to it. I mean, she's all for other people being comfortable with their feelings, but then goes around pretending everything's fine when it clearly isn't.

Anyway, when we got outside, Magenta was sitting on the steps all on her own. And she looked frozen.

'You OK?' I asked. 'Where's Spyro?'

She jumped up as though someone had just shot ten thousand volts of electricity through the step. 'Erm ...' Her eyes were darting all over the place, like she'd just been caught out. 'He wanted to stay longer, but I was really tired ... and ... I've got to help Belinda clean the house tomorrow,' she blustered.

Yeah, right! I might have been totally Pete Tong about this type of gig being Magenta's cup of tea, but I knew for a fact that there was no way she'd be going home at half past eleven because she needed to do housework tomorrow – only the promise of a year's free shopping at Up Front would entice her to even look at the Hoover. It was more likely Mr Super-ego Evangelides had ditched her.

'How're you getting home?' I asked, but before she could answer, she dodged behind my back, and ducked down as though she was hiding from someone.

'Don't say anything,' she whispered.

She was holding on to my T-shirt round my waist and, I hate to admit this when I was supposed to be with Jodi, but it felt kinda good having Magenta's hands on me again. Whoa! I stopped myself almost before the thought had finished running through my mind. What was wrong with me? Had I inherited the two-timing gene like my dad and my brother? I gave my head a little shake, to bring myself back to reality: this was Magenta – the girl who'd tied me in emotional knots for the last year and a half. There was no way I was going to allow myself to start having feelings for her again.

I kept my eyes straight ahead and spoke without moving my lips. 'Who're you trying to avoid?'

Just then Jodi looked over and waved to this rank kid from her tutor group. He's always gobbing in the quad and seems to have a nasal drip that's on permanent green.

'Hi, Pete! Did you enjoy it?' she called.

'Sssssh!' Magenta whispered. 'Don't let him see me.'

He came over and started talking to us. 'It was all right . . .' He made a rasping sound in his throat, as though he was trying to bring up a lungful of muck. 'But I lost my girlfriend right at the beginning and I never did find her.'

'Really?' I queried. He had a girlfriend? Who on earth would go out with that snot-meister? I tried to hide my disbelief by looking at my feet. 'Too bad. Anyone I know?' I asked, then felt a sharp prod in my lower back.

He wiped his nose across the sleeve of his hoody. (It had a slogan across the chest and was splattered with splashes of khaki but it was difficult to tell which was pattern and which was snot – gross!) Then he said, 'It's Magenta Orange. You know, from your year.'

'What?' Now that I was *not* expecting! Then, 'Owwww!' I screamed, as a finger bored into my kidney area.

'But I thought Magenta was going out with your brother . . .' Jodi began, then stopped and jolted as though she'd been goosed. 'Ouch!' she shrieked.

I put my arm round her waist and kissed her on the cheek. 'Sorry,' I said, trying to cover for Magenta. 'Just an affectionate little prod.' I moved my foot back to try and give Magenta a kick warning her to back off.

'Oh look, there's my brother's car. I'd better go,' Pete said, clearing his throat again and gobbing on to the steps. 'If you see Magenta, tell her I'm sorry I lost her and I'll catch up with her on Monday.'

'No problem,' I said.

As soon as he'd gone Magenta stood up and came round in front of us. 'Phew! That was a close one. Thank you sooooooo much. I have had a total nightmare tonight – I can't tell you! Anyway, I'm absolutely frozen. I couldn't cadge a lift home with you, could I? Cheers.'

Jodi narrowed her eyes. 'I thought you were going with Spyro?'

Magenta flapped her hand as though it was the most ridiculous suggestion ever. 'What, that arrogant pig? No way! Actually, it was a huge mix-up because I thought I was supposed to be with Spyro's *older* brother, Stavros, but when it turned out to be Pete – well, need I say more?'

Dr Plock dropped Magenta and me off and once I'd checked in with Mum, I went round and knocked on Magenta's French window.

'Anything you want to talk about?' I asked,

sitting on the end of her bed – I think Jodi's emo-thing is rubbing off on me.

Anyway, Magenta poured out the whole story. I always knew that Spyros Evangelides was a creep, but he'd taken the biscuit tonight. Poor Magenta! What a rat!

'Well, if it's any consolation,' I said, trying to cheer her up, 'I thought you looked nang in those hot pants.'

She gave me a puzzled look. 'Hot pants? They were my . . .' Then she stopped and smiled. 'Thanks, Daniel. It's nice to see that some people notice how much trouble I take with my accessorising.'

Even though Magenta and I are speaking again, I didn't really have much chance to talk to her during the week. Magnus was round every evening for us to put our track together again and we were in the Music Technology room every lunch time and break trying to repair the damage Spud had done.

There was no rehearsal on Saturday morning, although we had to go to the Youth Centre for the sound check before the concert in the evening.

As I was getting ready to go to my tutor's this morning, Mum appeared in my bedroom doorway. She was holding up three cards in one hand and a single rose that had been dyed black in the other. Then she did a sort of jazz hands thing with them and grinned.

'The postman's been,' she said, in that tone of voice she used to use at Christmas when Joe and I were little and she was trying to kid us that Santa had managed to manoeuvre himself through the central heating boiler.

I was stuffing books into my backpack. 'And?'

She looked at each envelope in turn. 'Mr Daniel Davis.' She tossed the card on to my bed. 'Daniel Davis.' A second one landed on my duvet. 'Danno. And . . .' she read the card attached to the rosebud, '. . . To Dan – Guess who?'

Yikes! I'd been so caught up in redoing our music that I'd completely forgotten that today was Valentine's Day. I picked up the first card: it was a funny cartoon one with a Manchester postmark – obviously from Justine. The second was in Arlette's handwriting; I'd recognise it anywhere. You'd have thought she'd at least have tried to disguise it. Worryingly, the third was totally off the slush scale and was clearly from Manky-Margaret, Dad's girlfriend's daughter. Oh boy – this crush thing was getting out of hand. I was going to have to have a word with Dad or it was going to have a serious impact on my contact visits.

I looked at the rose and felt a stab of guilt. Although the card wasn't signed, it didn't take a genius to work out that it was from Jodi. I felt as though some giant emotional concrete mixer had just dumped its load into my chest.

'I'd better get her one on the way back from Mr Dumbarton's,' I said.

But Mum just looked at me. Oh no! I recognised that expression. It's the one that she uses when she's going to launch into her Kitchen Sink Psychology for Dummies routine.

'Is that what you really want, Daniel? Because a card bought out of obligation is worse than no card at all.'

Oh great – pile on the guilt, why don't you! 'It's not obligation. I just don't want her to think that I've forgotten,' I explained.

'But you have.' Cheers, Mum – the first person to be awarded a PhD in Stating the Bleedin' Obvious.

'I've been busy all week,' I protested.

'And I'm suspecting that if you really cared about this Jodi girl, you would've remembered, regardless of how much work you had to do.' She nodded her head in this really annoying way that she has when she thinks she's right. 'I don't recall you ever forgetting to send Magenta a Valentine's card – even before you went out with her.'

What has Magenta got to do with anything? Why did she have to bring her into it?

'I need to go,' I said, feeling my level of comfort going way off the gauge.

As I walked to Mr D's I tried to put the conversation with Mum out of my head. I focused on the contest tonight and ran through our piece over and over in my mind. Magnus and I had worked our socks off this week and I was pleased with the finished result. Weird as it sounds, I think Spud did us a favour, wiping out our original track, because we've learned from our mistakes and the new one is wicked – much better than the first one ever was.

The music was going round my head and I was picturing all the slides flashing across the stage. Angus has got some indoor fireworks and rigged them up to go off for the finale. (I did get Magnus to check that he'd followed the instructions properly.)

As I neared Mr D's house, I found I was thinking about Magenta quite a lot too – not romantically, you understand, but I was thinking about her band Spangle Babes and how she's choreographed it. Because she's been coming to Mr D's every Saturday, I hadn't really seen her part in the band till last week, and you should've seen her dancing – she was brilliant.

As I reached the front door, I had a quick flashback to last night with Magenta up on the stage, launching herself into the crowd, and a smile began to form on my lips. I reached my hand out to press the bell, when the door burst open and Magenta was standing, spread-eagled across the doorway, looking terrified.

Her eyes were wide – and believe me, she has beautiful eyes – but this morning they looked wild and, if I'm honest, a tad scary. And her face was very pale. I thought maybe she wasn't feeling too good – or maybe she'd forgotten to put on her make-up. She looked like she'd seen a ghost.

'Are you OK?' I asked as she stumbled out on to the step and flung her arms round me.

'Daniel!' she quaked. 'He's dead. I've killed the Dung-beetle!'

Oh boy! She'd excelled herself this time.

13
Magenta

Ohmigod, ohmigod, ohmigod! The most terrible thing in the world has happened – I'm a murderer!

Because Dad's back (with a vengeance, I might add – so much for hoping that a spell away might have mellowed him), I had to go to the Dung-beetle's this morning for the duration of my whole two-hour sentence. Belinda had asked me to pick up some more sequins on the way – she's made me the most amazing sparkly hot pants for the contest tonight. Even though they're blue like the rest of Spangle Babes, they're gorgeous. And she's had my bodice cleaned too, so that I'm going to look soooooo sophisticated. Or I will if I'm not clapped in irons, rotting in a police cell somewhere.

Anyway, I called in at the wool shop on the High Street to buy the sequins and when I came out, I saw these furry mice toys in the pet shop next door. Old Mrs Pickles across the road found a stray kitten last week – he can't be more than four or five months old. Belinda helped her put posters up everywhere, but no one's claimed him yet, so I thought it would be nice to buy him one of the fluffy mice with what was left of Belinda's money.

I put it in my bag and forgot about it until almost the end of the lesson when the Dung-beetle was droning on about trigonometry and hypotenuse and other useless stuff that I will never need in my life – ever! Honestly, if I'd known that doing well in my exams meant being moved into the Higher Level Maths group, I'd never have bothered.

'The formulae are easy to remember, Magenta,' he said, shuffling up and down in his sloppy cardigan and evil slippers. 'Sin equals opposite over hypotenuse; cos equals adjacent over hypotenuse and tan equals opposite over adjacent.' Yeah – that is sooooo easy to remember – not! 'Which one you use depends entirely on the information given to you in the question.' Boooooring! He was making himself a cup of tea and was standing with his back to me as he went on, 'The acronym SOHCAHTOA – sock-a-toe-a – might help you to remember . . .' I looked at his health-hazard footwear and decided that anything to do with socks and toes was a no-no. In fact I was feeling distinctly queasy just thinking about them. '. . . or the mnemonic: some old horse cracked all his teeth on acorns . . .' Nim nim nim! Horses? Acorns? Who cares? Feed it on grass then if it keeps breaking its teeth on the hard stuff.

I was in imminent danger of brain-death, so I reached down into my bag and got out the furry mouse that I'd bought for Mrs Pickles' kitten. When I was little, Dad used to press my teddies down at the back and somehow make them jump along the table, so that it looked as though they were really moving. (OK – give me a break – I was only about four at the time!) I decided to have a go with the furry mouse, pressing it just above its tail and then letting go. At first, it didn't do anything. The second time, it executed a fairly creditable back flip, and then, just as the Dung-beetle turned round, I must have hit it in the right place because it leapt about twenty centimetres across the table – completely clearing my maths book. Wow! How impressive was that?

Obviously not to the Dung-beetle though, because . . . uh-oh! His face went from its normal sickly yellow colour to a more disgusting shade of grey. Then his knees just folded under him and he fell on to the nylon mat in front of the sink, cracking his head on the edge of the draining board as he went down.

Oh no! I was frozen in horror. I held my breath waiting for him to get up and give me an earbashing. But he didn't.

'Mr Dumbarton?' I said. 'Are you all right?'

Nothing! He just lay on the floor not moving or anything. Then a massive puddle of blood started to spread out across the lino.

'Sir? Speak to me, sir.'

And the awful truth dawned on me – he was dead.

Oh my God! What had I done? I'd killed him! And the worst thing was, everyone knew I didn't like him, so the police were bound to think that it was deliberate. Even though there must be a gazillion less drastic ways of getting rid of a boring teacher than murder, I was going to get blamed. Because . . . well just because I always get blamed for everything. I was going to be another statistic – the subject of one of those documentaries about innocent people who've been sent down for crimes they didn't commit. I was going to spend the rest of my days living in Cell Block H and surviving on porridge (which I hate, by the way). It was the end of my life as I knew it!

I had to do something. I had to run – escape before anyone suspected me. No, I wasn't thinking straight:

1. My legs were shaking uncontrollably: I could barely even walk, let alone run.

2. Where was I going to run to? Godzilla (aka my dad) would turn me over to the police – no questions asked. And, apart from my cousins from hell in Manchester (who would also turn me in without batting a single panda-fied eyelid), I didn't have any other family.

And,

3. Now I'd bought the stupid mouse toy, I didn't even have enough money on me to get the bus into town, let alone the train to anywhere.

I had no option but to do the decent thing and come clean – but first I needed to call for assistance.

'Help!' I shouted – well, whimpered really, because it seemed like my throat had gone into spasm. You see, that's what happens to the wicked – they get punished!

Even though my legs were still in the jelly

stage of fright, I managed to stagger to the door. And what a relief when I opened it! Believe me, I have never been so pleased to see Daniel as I was at that moment.

'Daniel!' I spluttered. 'He's dead. I've killed the Dung-beetle!'

And, you should've seen him – he was like Superman the way he took charge and handled everything in such a firm and commanding way. He's not Health and Safety Rep of the stage crew for nothing!

'Phone 999 and get an ambulance,' he ordered, walking straight past me into the house.

'What about the police?' I asked, running after him. 'Shouldn't I hand myself in?'

'Let's establish the facts first,' he said – just like one of those old-fashioned detectives on afternoon TV.

And he was right because, guess what? When we got back into the kitchen, the Dung-beetle was only sitting up with his back against the cupboards. He was alive! Phew – I cannot tell you how relieved I was not to be up on a murder charge. OK, so there was blood gushing down his face, but he was upright (almost) and breathing again.

'You've been resurrected!' I yelled, running over to him and doing the unmentionable – yes, I actually hugged him. Ewww! Who'd ever have thought that I'd have made any form of contact with the Dung-beetle, let alone a full-on hug. Relief does strange things to people.

'Mind my head!' he spluttered. Ooops! Then he started to mumble, 'There was a mouse . . .' Oh boy! I'd been hoping my mouse acrobatics and his fainting fit had been purely coincidental. 'I've been phobic about rodents since I was a child . . .' *Now* he tells me! 'I'm so sorry, Magenta. I didn't mean to frighten you.'

'No worries . . .' I started, but then there was this strange uncomfortable feeling in my tummy, like I'd eaten something that didn't quite agree with me. I tried to swallow it down, but it kept sticking there. I don't know what it was, but it just didn't seem right to let him think that he was the bad guy in all this. So – and I know you're probably going to find this a little difficult to believe – my conscience only went and got the better of me.

'Actually, it was *my* mouse,' I confessed.

And it paid off because Daniel and I went in the ambulance with him to hospital and while we were waiting in A & E two amazing things happened.

1. Cyril – as Mr Dumbarton says Daniel and I can now call him (I've decided not to use that other name any more, because it's really not very nice – although, apparently, Daniel says that dung-beetles were considered sacred in Ancient Egypt. But, as we're not living in Ancient Egypt and, even though he might have come back from the dead, I think referring to Cyril as sacred is going a teensy bit too far – I'm just going to stick to his real name). Anyway, Cyril said that he considered two hours was too long for me to maintain concentration, so he was going to tell Dad that it would be better for me to only have a one-hour session from now on. Yes! How's that for a result!

And:

2. As we were waiting for Cyril to be stitched up, Daniel put his arm round my shoulder – just in a friendly, reassuring way of course – nothing romantic. He said, 'You know, Magenta, I was really impressed with the way you told the truth back there. You could've just hidden the mouse and got

away with it, but you didn't and that shows real maturity. I was proud of you.' Then he gave me a kiss on the forehead – which was sooooo lovely, and I must admit, there was the teensiest hint of tinglage going on in my tummy area. But we're just going to be friends – and I'm absolutely, one hundred and seventy-nine per cent OK with that.

So you see, this *being the bigger person* thing really does work! Now all I have to do is get home and help Belinda finish sewing the sequins on to my hot pants, then be at the sound check at the Youth Centre at four o'clock.

Oooo! A sound check – how exciting is that? I'm starting to get nervous already.

14
Daniel & Magenta

Daniel

I can't believe I let myself fall for her stupid, childish tactics – again! She was all over me this afternoon when she thought she'd done Cyril in and needed my help. You should've seen her in A & E, creeping up to me and rubbing my arm and telling me how grateful she was – same old same old!

Of course, what does Danno the Gullible do? I believe her. In I went – head first at the deep end, allowing myself to fantasise about the fact that she'd finally grasped this whole maturity thing and we might be able to get it on again. Jeez, you'd think I'd have learnt by now. Talk about stupid alert!

We went to the sound check together and were both on a total high afterwards; Magenta because she hadn't made a single mistake in the routine and me because Bruno, the Youth Leader, has changed the line-up. Greg has to leave early because he's got a classical recital tonight as well, so Bruno's put Spiral Thrust in the first half and made Luminance the headline band. Which is über wicked!

When Magenta and I walked home afterwards she was all, 'I'll see you tonight – headliner!' And she leaned across and gave me a kiss on my cheek. Actually, it was a really cute little kiss that just brushed my skin, but it sent an electric current the size of the national grid down my spine. 'Good luck – and may the best girls win!' she'd teased.

'Yeah right!' And we'd both laughed as she went indoors.

Ggggrrr! I was so convinced Magenta and I were going to get back together again, I almost ended it with Jodi Plock! I can't believe I've been such a div. I should've known better than to even think for a nanosecond that she meant any of it. I'd get better odds on a snowman crossing the Sahara on rollerblades than Magenta actually keeping her word. Angus was right: I am well out of it.

Tonight, just before the contest started, Magnus and I were in the wings setting up the computer and sound module on a trolley, so that we could just wheel it on to the stage for our set.

I was looking round for Magenta, but I couldn't see her anywhere.

The dhol drummers were the opening band and were waiting for Bruno to announce them but there were still a few family and friends arriving, shuffling in at the back. I had a peek and couldn't believe it – the Youth Centre was rammed; standing room only!

I thought that Magenta hadn't arrived yet because Spangle Babes weren't on till about halfway through, although Arlette was by the side of the stage draped all over Jac Dhillon as he waited to go on. Then, suddenly, Arlette's mobile bleeped.

'I told you – all mobiles should be off!' Bruno warned.

Arlette gave an apologetic smile. 'Sorry.' But she carried on reading the message anyway, then gasped and started to make a call.

'I said, OFF! Or I'll take it away till the end of the concert,' Bruno said in this sort of hushed bellow.

Arlette turned off her phone with a tut, and Bruno walked out on to the stage to introduce the first act.

'Ladies and gentlemen, brothers and sisters, grannies and granddads, welcome to Battle of the

Bands . . .' I heard him begin. He went on to say a lot of stuff about the judges: one of them was a mate of his who plays in a reggae band, another was a jazz singer, there was a woman who does amateur operatics and Ms Keyes had also agreed to be a judge – which I think was pretty decent of her. Then after a couple of minutes, I heard Bruno say, '. . . so I am delighted to introduce our first band of the evening. Please give it up for – MaSikhs!'

Jac, Sundeep and the others started drumming as they walked out and the whole place erupted with applause. Oh crump! This was it! This was what all the planning and hard work had been for. My stomach felt like someone had wrapped it in rubber bands and my palms started to sweat. Great! That was all I needed – sweaty hands as I was trying to do the live effects on our track!

I closed my eyes and took a deep breath to try and calm my nerves but I was snapped back to reality when Arlette stormed across to where Magnus and I were standing guard over the computer – a preventative measure to ensure that Spud couldn't get within cocking-up distance of our equipment.

'Daniel – what happened between you and Madge today, because I've just got a text to say she's not coming?' Whoa! That was the harshest whisper I've ever heard.

'What!' I was shocked; in fact, I might as well have been told that the bottom had fallen out of my world. 'What do you mean, she's not coming?' In my head, I'd allowed myself to imagine Magenta and me standing in the wings, holding hands and cheering each other on. OK, so I know there was the minor detail of ending it with Jodi, but I hadn't really had a chance yet. And now Arlette's news had hit me like the Sledgehammer of Disappointment – smack in the middle of my chest. Although I wasn't sure why she seemed to be dumping Magenta's no-show on me. 'Anyway . . .' I was speaking very low, partly so that she couldn't tell how upset I was and also so that my voice didn't carry on to the stage and disturb MaSikhs. 'This is my fault – why?'

'Because it always is where Madge is concerned.' I couldn't believe this was the girl who'd sent me a Valentine this morning. If she was supposed to fancy me, she had a funny way of showing it. 'And I don't know why she's not coming; she's just sent her usual excuse about Belinda going into labour – again!'

'Well, F Y I, nothing happened between us today,' I hissed. 'And anyway, she can hardly help it if the baby's coming.' My disappointment was replaced with a smidge of hope that she had a genuine reason for not turning up and a buzz of excitement that she would soon have her little brother or sister.

'Oh yeah – like that's what's really happened! She's been using that old chestnut for months. It's more likely that someone's upset her and she's bottled out,' Arlette went on. 'She's even turned off her phone and the landline's engaged.'

And that's when the pieces started to fall into place. Arlette might be right – I could recall at least three other occasions when Magenta had said that Belinda had gone into labour – and that's when we've hardly been speaking for the past six weeks, so heaven knows how many times she's said it to other people! In fact she was probably sitting at home now, throwing a hissy fit because her costume wasn't diva enough, or her hair was too crinkly, or her make-up didn't look right.

A wave of irritation welled up inside me. If

Magenta hadn't got the guts to perform with her own band, she could at least have come along to support them – and me! How selfish could you get? Well, she'd played me for a fool for the last time. I'm better off without her and I've got more important things to worry about than some spoilt little princess who needs to be the centre of attention all the time: I needed to focus on our performance tonight.

Magenta

Eeeewww! Seriously – I mean it! I am never having children – EVER!

We were just about to go out of the door for the concert tonight, when Belinda only went and peed her pants like that woman in the hospital did. Talk about timing! She could've waited a few hours till after the Battle of the Bands. But, oh no, she had to choose tonight of all times.

Of course I knew it was the whole water-breaking thing – been there, seen it, watched the entire maternity team sweep into action – so I wasn't freaked out by what was going on in the Belinda department; it was Dad that was doing my head in.

'Oh good God! Don't move!' he cried, staring at this pool of liquid on the hall floor.

'Couldn't if I wanted to,' Belinda gasped, bending forwards and taking really fast breaths.

Dad was pacing up and down the hall. 'Call the midwife! Call an ambulance! Lie down! Do something!'

Belinda and I looked at each other. 'Who's he talking to?' I asked.

Belinda shrugged – well, ish – she was still clutching the end of the stairs, doing this funny breathing. Then she stood up and, amazingly, she looked completely normal again, like nothing had happened. 'Would you be a darling, Magenta, and pop upstairs to fetch the midwife's number out of my bag, please?'

I checked my watch; it was almost seven o'clock – still time to get to the Battle of the Bands before it started – if I was quick.

'The number's here,' Dad said, rushing past her to the phone and snatching a piece of paper from under it.

'No, that's Siobhan's number, the old midwife – she's got a ruptured appendix. I got a call this morning. The number for the on-call midwife is in my bag – oooohhh!' And she doubled over again and did her panty-breathing thing.

'What!' Dad shrieked.

'Don't worry,' I tried to reassure them both. 'We did about this in PSE and first babies always take ages. You might be having pains for days. I'll just get the number then I'll be off to the Youth Centre.'

Belinda and Dad both looked at each other and then at me. 'Actually,' Belinda sighed, lowering herself on to the bottom stair, 'this isn't a first baby.'

'Huh?' I couldn't believe what I was hearing. 'You mean I've got a stepsister or brother somewhere that I didn't know about?' How could they keep this from me? My family tree is pretty pathetic compared to everyone else's in my class, so another sibling (even a step-one) would've boosted it big time.

'No.' Belinda shook her head and looked sad. 'It was six years ago, in my last relationship. I had a little boy, but he was very ill and didn't survive.'

Last to know again! I felt really hurt. I'd been halfway upstairs to get the phone number but I sat down too. 'Why didn't you tell me?'

'Because that sort of information is on a need-to-know basis. Ooooohhhh!' Belinda pursed her lips and began panting again. When she stopped, she went on, 'And you only need to know now, because this little one isn't hanging around.' She rubbed her tummy.

Uh-oh! 'You mean . . . ?'

'Just get the midwife's number, Magenta – now!' Dad yelled.

Whoa! No need to take it out on me! I ran upstairs and fetched Belinda's bag, but when Dad tried to ring the number, the answerphone came on.

'I thought this was supposed to be a twenty-four-hour service!' His decibel level was approaching the range that could permanently damage hearing.

Whereas, Belinda was being amazingly calm about everything. 'It is. She'll call back, don't worry.'

'Don't worry? You've gone into labour two weeks early and not a midwife in sight and you tell me not to worry!' he said, picking up Belinda's coat. 'Right, that's it – get in the car; we're going to the hospital.'

Belinda had started to make her way back along the hall towards the sitting room. But at the word 'hospital' she turned on him. Uh-oh – I sensed a domestic coming on.

'I am not having this baby in that place,' she snapped. 'Merlin was born in hospital and I am not going through that again. This baby will be born at home – is that ... ooooohhhh!' She grabbed the door jamb and doubled over again.

Merlin? Oh dear Lord! I know Belinda's a bit of a mythology geek, but what if she wants to call this one something Arthurian, like Guinevere, or Lancelot? How can I ever do big-sisterly things like take it to the swings and have to call: *Come here, Excalibur!*

'All right, all right. We'll stay here,' Dad conceded. Jeez, I wish he'd give in to *me* that easily. 'I'll get the birthing pool set up. Magenta, give me a hand, will you?'

OK, there seemed to be a minor detail that had escaped his notice here – i.e. I was wearing a silver bodice and sparkly hot pants. Which, unless I'm massively mistaken, is *not* your average midwifery attire. In fact, it was a pretty huge clue to the fact that I was supposed to be at the Battle of the Bands ... I checked my watch: oh, great – right now!

Daniel

'You all right, babe?' Jodi slung her arm round my shoulder and kissed me on the cheek. 'Angus said you wanted to speak to me.'

Cheers, Angus! That'll teach me to keep my big mouth shut about finishing with someone. There's a back room at the Youth Centre, it's usually the quiet room, but tonight it was being used as a holding area and most of the acts were in there – Angus and Spud included. Magnus and I had been stationed in the wings throughout the contest, just in case some marauding lunatic tried to mess with our music (no names mentioned, but Spud had been banned from coming within five metres of the stage/wings area until we went on).

'Sssh!' I whispered to Jodi, pointing to where Spiral Thrust were performing their set. This was hardly the time to be dumping someone.

She shrugged and walked away again. I felt a wave of relief; I couldn't be doing with all this girl stuff at the moment. I needed to concentrate tonight.

It was great to have such a good view of all the other bands as they went on, but it was also nerve-racking watching the opposition from close quarters. I was so nervous, I felt like a whole battalion of soldier ants was on manoeuvres in my stomach. And I was so twitchy, I couldn't keep my hands and feet still for a second.

'What do you think?' I whispered to Magnus, inclining my head towards the stage.

Magnus nodded. 'I don't like the geezer, but that Spyro certainly knows how to work a drum kit.'

Spyro was standing on his stool, with one foot on the bass drum, crashing the cymbals in a frenzy, while Gregory did this amazing guitar riff – you should've seen the speed of his fingers on the strings.

The audience were going wild for them. I felt sick.

Magenta

Who invented stupid birthing pools? There's about five thousand wooden panels (well, eight, actually) that are all supposed to slot into these upright bits to make an octagon. Then you fit the plastic liner into the frame. Yeah – great theory! Shame all the 'identical' sides aren't actually identical! It's like one of those wooden puzzles I had to do when Dad and Gran took me to an educational psychologist in

Year 7. 'See if you can make these nine hundred little pieces into one big ball as fast as you can.' Then she had the stopwatch of doom ticking away as I did it. Of course it was all über-stressful because I knew that if I didn't do it in a certain time they'd send me off to the Portakabin with people like Perry Proctor and Billy O'Dowd. And the adults thought *I* had a problem!

But speaking of über-stress; tonight, our particular stopwatch of doom was Belinda, kneeling on all fours, panting and groaning at scarily decreasing intervals. And, if I wasn't mistaken, the length of the panting and groaning sessions was scarily *in*creasing! Now, I'm no expert on childbirth, but I've watched enough films to know that that was a pretty sure sign that the baby was coming – midwife or no midwife!

Of course Dad didn't help by ranting, 'Where's that bloody midwife?' every couple of minutes.

The instructions for the pool came on a DVD, but we'd had to take the TV out of the sitting room so that the birthing pool would fit in. And every time Dad made to go to the kitchen to see what to do next, Belinda let out a wail: 'Don't leave me!'

So, no pressure on me then!

Daniel

Spangle Babes were lined up ready to go on. I'd been trying to avoid thinking about Magenta all evening but when I saw them all in their blue and silver outfits, looking totally off the hinges, I felt a pang of sadness that she wasn't here with them.

'Good luck!' I gave the girls the thumbs-up as they walked out on stage.

I knew how much this had meant to Magenta. And watching them singing together and dancing to the moves she'd created and wearing the costumes she'd designed, it felt wrong that she wasn't here to be part of it. In my heart, I suspected that Arlette was right and she was probably sulking at home, but I wanted to give her one last chance.

'Don't move,' I whispered to Magnus. 'I just need to go out for a minute.'

As I stood outside the Youth Centre, I could hear the crowd clapping and shouting at the end of Spangle Babes' routine. I dialled Magenta's mobile but, as Arlette had said, it was switched off. Then I tried the landline but it just rang and rang until the answerphone came on. Either she'd gone out somewhere else, or she was sitting at home in a strop, avoiding all calls. But whatever the reason, it was a pretty immature thing to do.

'Hi, babe. Magnus said you'd be out here.' Jodi kissed me on the lips. 'We're on next and it'd be really cool if you were there to watch me.'

I didn't know if I wanted to be with Jodi or keep hanging on for Magenta. Either way, I'd be a total rat to ditch Jodi just before she went on stage. I flipped my phone shut.

'Sure!' I said, and we walked back into the hall.

Magenta

Great! Just what I need – the phone rings just when I've got Dad's watch in one hand (timing Belinda's contractions) and the hosepipe in the other, filling up the birthing pool.

'Give me the hose and you go and answer the phone,' Dad said, wiping the sweat off his forehead like he'd been down the gym or something. Honestly, from where I was standing it seemed like it was Belinda doing all the work. All he'd been doing was rubbing her back and singing stupid songs. 'Hurry up – it might be the midwife!' he snapped.

Cheek! I think there are some people who really shouldn't go in for parenthood, and Dad is definitely one of them. Anyway, I was too late. I'd just got to the phone when it went on to answerphone and the person rang off.

'Do 1471!' Dad shouted from the front room.

But I didn't get the chance because just at that moment the doorbell rang. And hallelujah – not before time – it was the midwife!

'I'm so sorry,' she blustered. 'I was on another delivery and then there was a terrible traffic jam on the ring road.' She took off her coat and handed it to me, then peeled off an enormous scarf. 'Now, where's your mother?'

I thought that was a pretty insensitive question and wasn't quite sure what relevance my mother had to the current situation. 'Er . . . dead,' I said.

'What?' She dropped her bag and staggered backwards. 'Oh, Jesus, Joseph and Mary! Why on earth didn't you call an ambulance?'

'Because I was only three at the time?' I ventured.

She stood up and cocked her head on one side. 'I am at the right house . . . ?' But another wail from Belinda answered her question. 'Right,' she said, marching into the front room. 'Let's see how Mummy's doing.'

The pool was quite full, so I was given the job of winding up the hose and making cups of tea for Dad and the midwife. See what I mean about not ever having any babies – Belinda's doing all the hard graft in there and the others are getting all the perks!

I put the kettle on and looked at the clock in the kitchen: it was almost ten o'clock. The Battle of the Bands would be nearing its climax by now. I wondered how Spangle Babes had done and whether or not they'd missed me. I tried to phone Arlette and Seema but both their phones were off. As the headline act, Daniel would be going on soon, so I tried to phone him, too. But then I remembered at the sound check Bruno had told us all to turn off our phones so as not to interfere with the audio equipment.

I sighed. It probably sounds silly, but the Battle of the Bands had meant so much to me, yet, when I thought about what was going on in the next room – the competition really didn't matter at all. What mattered was that my little baby brother or sister was coming into the world right now – and I'd been part of it.

I pulled the hose-attachment off the tap in the

kitchen and coiled the hosepipe round my elbow and up over my thumb, till the whole thing was wound into one enormous loop, then I went to put it back in the garden shed. But, uh-oh! As I opened the shed door, Sirius darted between my legs and headed for the house. Oh no! I'd forgotten that Dad had given strict instructions for him to stay in the shed till after Belinda had had the baby.

'Bad dog! Come back!' I yelled. But he was into the kitchen and through the door to the hall faster than you could say *Road Runner*! 'Sirius, stop!' I shouted, running after him.

I caught up with him in the hall, just as he was nosing open the front-room door.

'Gotcha!' I said, reaching down to pick him up. Unfortunately, I still had the coiled hose over one arm and, as I bent down, the nozzle end slipped off and whacked Sirius right on the nose. He gave a yelp and sprang through the door as though he'd been bitten by a rattlesnake.

'Get him out of here!' Dad was standing at one end of the pool holding Belinda (who was wearing nothing but a long white T-shirt) and lowering her into the water.

I lurched at Sirius, but he jumped up on to the

settee out of reach. Unfortunately, as I lunged forward, my foot caught the nozzle of the hosepipe and I went over on my ankle. I tripped up and, despite my best efforts to break my fall on the midwife, I crashed sideways into the edge of the birthing pool. Ouch! It caught me on the ribs and really hurt.

But, honestly, it just goes to show what a silly idea birthing pools are, because just a teensy little knock like that had dislodged one of the panels. And it had taken Dad and me ages to put together – in fact some of my pieces wouldn't fit in the slots at all and I'd just had to prop them up with Dad's speakers while he was rubbing Belinda's back at the other side of the room. But the liner still fitted all right, so it hadn't made it any less watertight.

Until now! The weight of me hitting the edge of the pool had made a tidal wave of water slop against the panel by the speaker and the whole section started to lean outwards. Ooops! Water began to cascade over the top on to Dad's speaker and then spill on to the floor. Dad and the midwife were both glaring at me like it was my fault but, honestly, if the sections had slotted into the uprights better, none of this would've happened. How substandard is that?

I don't think Belinda noticed because she was sticking her tongue out and panting like Sirius does when he's hot. And, speaking of Sirius, I think he must've been a duck in a former life, because he loves water and chose that moment to launch himself off the settee and into the birthing pool.

'MAGENTAAAAAAAA!' Dad growled as the impact of Sirius caused the panel to collapse altogether and water slooshed on to his feet.

'Waaagh!' wailed the midwife.

Sirius seemed to be the only one enjoying himself as he surfed the torrent of water cascading on to the sitting-room floor.

'Oooooooohhhhhh!' Belinda let out a long moan. 'I think it's coming!'

Uh-oh!

Daniel

Magnus and I wheeled our trolley on to the stage. My mouth was as dry as the Gobi Desert in a sandstorm. I kept licking my lips but, even though I'd got a bottle of water with me, I didn't dare drink anything – I'd been peeing with nerves all evening.

The lights went down. The whole place was silent.

I opened the file and felt a tingle of excitement run down my spine. Our opening bar resonated through the hall and, simultaneously, images flashed up on a massive screen at the back of the stage and across the seating area. People started cheering and clapping to the beat. Wow! The atmosphere was electric.

Magnus and I worked together, adding live echo and reverb effects as well as samples to the track we'd laid down. It was pumping and everyone was bouncing up and down in their seats. What a buzz!

Gradually we increased the tempo, building up to a crescendo and, right on cue, Angus set off his fireworks. The effect was mind-blowing and the whole hall erupted in applause.

My heart was pounding and I had a grin like a half moon on my face that I couldn't control. Magnus and I stepped forward to take our bow.

'I'd also like to thank our technical support,' I said, beckoning Angus on to the stage. I looked round and Spud was peering out from the curtains, so I indicated for him to come out too – after all, if he hadn't messed up the first track, we'd never have created this one.

People were standing up and cheering and clapping. It was amazing. I looked round and saw Jodi in the wings; she gave me the thumbs-up. My eyes scanned the rest of the people backstage, hoping that Magenta might have turned up right at the last minute. Then I looked out into the crowd again – maybe she'd been in the audience all along.

After we'd wheeled our equipment off, Bruno addressed the audience.

'Ladies and gentlemen, I'm sure you'll agree we have a wealth of talent in our midst and it's going to take the judges a few minutes to make their decision. The bands tonight will be judged, not on spectacle, but on their whole performance – musical ability, stage presence – including appearance – and entertainment value . . .' I felt a lump the size of a basketball in my throat. If we'd been judged on spectacle, we'd have won hands down, but Magnus and I hadn't even thought about our stage presence and appearance. And, technically speaking, did ours constitute musical ability?

I needed to pee again!

Magenta

Dad carried Belinda up to the bedroom and he said I've got to start clearing up the house. Gran gets back tomorrow and she'll go ape if she sees this lot. I don't think even another grandchild will soften the blow!

There's lots of groaning wafting down from up there. I hope everything's all right.

Daniel

I was pacing up and down the back room with the rest of the bands. Spud and Angus were with us, so I knew they couldn't be doing any damage anywhere. No one was speaking. The only sound was Spyro nervously tapping out a drumbeat on the arm of one of the chairs.

Jodi came over and broke the silence. 'You never did tell me what it was you wanted to talk to me about. Is now a good time?'

Yeah, right – she wanted me to dump her in public? Not a good idea. But, actually, I needed to ask myself if I was actually going to dump her? When I'd watched Dead Petals on stage, she was really amazing: cute, sexy, talented and – let's not forget – very hot! I looked at her and she gave me a smile – and there you have it! Jodi's a great girl, but the bottom line is – she's not Magenta!

'OK – everybody on stage please,' Bruno called from the doorway. 'The judges have made their decision.'

Oh boy – this was it!

P.S.
Magenta

You know I hardly ever cry? Well – Oh! My! God! I haven't stopped blubbing for hours. This is the most moving thing – EVER!

I've got a little baby sister! And when I say, little, I mean tiny! She's minute! With teensy little fingers and teensy little toes – ten of each – I checked! And they've all got tiny weeny little nails on the end – just like a real human being. She's got this cute little turned-up nose and all this mad curly hair – which means she's obviously going to have my problem with the frizz factor! Although Belinda tells me it might all fall out and grow back straight – phew! But even if it doesn't, I'll still love her. I'll just buy her her own hair straighteners for her first birthday! She's so cute; not at all like those baby dolls I used to play with when I was little. She's – well . . . real! I know I said I was never going to have children, but you can rewind on that one because I can't wait till I'm an adult and have one of my own!

She was born at quarter past eleven last night and she's called Indigo Valentine Lovell Orange – Indigo Orange for short! My sister; Indigo. May I introduce you to my sister; Indigo? This is my little sister, Indigo! Magenta and Indigo Orange. How fabulous does that sound?

As soon as she was born I phoned all my mates and told them. Daniel came straight round after the Battle of the Bands. He was so sweet. And guess what? He brought me some gift vouchers because I'd only gone and won *two* prizes! Can you believe it? And I wasn't even there! Well, it was the band that won them really, but considering that they were for best choreography and best costume, I think I'm totally justified in taking the credit.

Spangle Babes came third in the whole contest, which wasn't bad when you think they didn't have me in the line-up. MaSikhs were second and – Luminance won! I was so pleased for Daniel. Spiral Thrust didn't get anywhere and Daniel said Spyro was shouting out, 'Fix!' and kicking the amps and everything – what a plum!

Dad's gone off to pick up Gran and Auntie Venice from the airport this morning and Belinda's having a sleep, so Daniel and I are looking after

Indigo. We're having to sit in my bedroom because the front room still needs to dry out. Belinda said to leave her in her crib but I can't stop cuddling her; she's sooooooo gorgeous – even though she is still a bit prune-ified.

'She's got your eyes,' Daniel said, leaning across and stroking her minuscule little fingers.

'How can you tell?' I asked. 'They're closed most of the time.'

'I just can.' Just then Indigo gave this squeaky little meow sound and blinked open her eyes. 'You see, she looks just like you.'

'She does, actually,' I smiled, and gave her a little kiss on the forehead. 'Stick with me, sis. I have sooooooooo much to teach you!'

Then Daniel moved his hand up to my chin and gently turned me to face him. 'I'm so sorry about what happened at Christmas,' he said. 'Do you think we can start again?'

'Wow! I did not see that coming!' I gasped. Oh, all right then – I *did* see it coming but there was no way I was going to let Daniel know that. I didn't want to appear too keen – especially after I'd gone to all the trouble of forging Arl's handwriting on the Valentine card I sent him. I pretended to think about it for a moment. 'Maybe – but what about Jodi Plock?'

He shook his head. 'Jodi's history. You know there's never been anyone for me but you, Magenta.' How romantic was that? He looked down at Indigo again. 'And, even though we have our ups and downs, I've always thought that we'd be together for ever, you know – maybe one day settle down and have one of these of our own.' He placed his finger into Indigo's tiny curled-up fist. 'What do you think?'

Oh my God! This I *really* hadn't seen coming! 'You mean we could be like one of those ancient couples you see in the paper who've been together for a billion years and were childhood sweethearts?'

'Sounds good to me,' he said, brushing his lips against mine – taking care not to squash Indigo of course.

'OK,' I agreed, 'but on one condition.'

Daniel smiled. 'Go on.'

'I want to keep my own name.' I've been talking to Belinda and she explained that the reason she's still Belinda Lovell is that the days when wives were the property of their husbands has long gone and she's an independent person in her own right.

'OK,' Daniel smiled. 'If that's what you want.'

I laid Indigo down in the crib and turned to face him. 'Thank you,' I said, pulling him towards me and giving him a proper kiss.

So, all in all, I've had quite an eventful week:

1. Belinda bought me an amazing new phone to replace the one I lost at the concert,
2. I got a reprieve from a murder charge,
3. I won prizes for best costume and best choreographer,
4. I've got a new baby sister
5. And a new boyfriend (well an old one revamped but that still counts)

And best of all, I'm going to be Magenta Orange – for ever!

A Note from Magenta

Name: Magenta Olivia Orange (OK, OK, so now you know why I NEVER have my full initials on my science overall!)

Birthday: August 18th

Star Sign: Leo – sunny nature and sparkling personality, that's me. Although I'm not sure about the bit where it says Leos like to be the centre of attention – I don't think that fits for me at all, do you?

Fave colour: Magenta – of course! Preferably with sparkly bits. But failing that, any variation of pink

Fave food: Pizza – especially the Good King Wenceslas special – deep pan, crisp and even – get it?

Fave teacher: Get real! Those are two words that should never appear in the same sentence

Fave books: all the ones about me! *Magenta Orange* (where I have my first kiss – oh my God! What a nightmare!), *Magenta in the Pink* (where we do Archimedes High's answer to High School Musical), *Magenta Goes Green* (more trauma at the school summer camp), *Shades of Magenta* (which is all about my holiday last year) and, of course, this one!

And you can read even more about me on my blog:
http://magentaorange.blogspot.com/